Something BORROWED

A DARK, FORBIDDEN, AGE GAP, KIDNAPPING, MAFIA ROMANCE

HANNAH RIO

Something Borrowed

A DARK, FORBIDDEN, AGE GAP, KIDNAPPING, MAFIA ROMANCE

HANNAH RIO

HANNAH RIO

Copyright © 2024 by Hannah Rio

All rights reserved.

No part of this book may be reproduced in any form or by any electronic or mechanical means, including information storage and retrieval systems, without written permission from the author, except for the use of brief quotations in a book review.

A Note From Hannah

Some Hannah Rio titles may contain triggers, please read with caution, and look after your mental health.

Sign up to her newsletter here:
subscribepage.io/NKn98Z

CHAPTER ONE
Verity

The club is packed tonight. Pulsing and high energy. The vibe is buzzing.

I'm at the bar with my friends and we are all looking in the same direction.

At him.

He's so fucking tall it's impossible not to notice him. I know exactly who is. Rufino Vece. The enemy. The big, scary, dangerous man who I need to stay away from because our families have been at each other's throats for decades. But my amazing friends have just dared me to do something stupid and I'm always up for that.

I grin, putting my hand on my hip and tilting my head to the side.

"Ok, fine. I'll do it." I shout over the throbbing pulse of heavy bass blasting around us. My friends stare at me in horror. Sammy gasps and shakes her head, a mild look of panic in her eyes.

Of course, they underestimated me. They thought I'd never agree to it. I should not have agreed.

I turn towards the man they've challenged me to kiss, but one of my friends reaches out and grabs my arm. "Are you crazy? You father will kill you, what if it lands up on socials or something? He's dangerous." Dante says, his eyes wide with shock. He tugs me towards him and shakes his head.

They are all laughing, drunk and causing shit. But I am right there in the zone with them. We are always causing shit. This is nothing new.

"So what if he's my dad's enemy?" I shrug my shoulders, still grinning, my eyes narrowed.

"Do it." Bella shouts, throwing her arm in the air and spilling her drink.

"Don't be a dumbass." Dante sniggers. He won't let me go. It's a cautious warning.

I roll my eyes. *"Fine*, let's get another round then." They shouldn't challenge me if they don't want me to go through with it. You would think they know me better by now.

Dante waves the bartender over to order another round of tequilas.

He leans across the bar to pull the bowl of lemon slices closer.

I'm still watching Rufino Vece. Fuck - he is *hot*. Like wickedly divine. He's leaning against the bar counter in his fitted black suit and his eyes are on me. I smirk at him and wink across the bar. His expression doesn't change. I can feel the danger oozing off him like dark syrup.

I lick my lips. I would love to play a few games with him. The more forbidden the fruit, the sweeter it tastes - or so I've been told.

He's tall, and his dark red hair and piercing green eyes are captivating. I want him. But I can't have him.

But I do like a challenge.

While he is watching me, he rolls his sleeves up over his forearms and I think he's flirting back.

"Hey, are you daydreaming or what?" Dante shouts, grabbing my attention and handing me the shot of tequila.

I take it from him, and all of my friends yell *cheers* before we tip our heads back. The alcohol burns down my throat and into my chest.

Honestly, my friends are a terrible influence. I mean, I'm not much better, but whenever I hang out with them, we get into trouble.

I think tonight is going to be no different because now they've put this idea in my head. I can't seem to get rid of it. Not even the tequila is diluting the thoughts.

I want the Red Vece. It's *only* because I can't have him.

I *want* to accept this challenge. It's like an evil seed in my mind that's taken root, and now it will be impossible to let go.

Bella, Dante, and Sammy head towards the dance floor and drag me along with them. Pulling me away from the bar and away from his intense stare.

Music vibrates through my body and I forget about the red-haired Viking for a while - getting lost in the enjoyment and freedom of dancing and letting go.

It's cooking in the club and my short, bright blue dress is sticking to my body.

I need a breather and some fresh air. Or another drink. Either way, I'm melting.

I signal my friends and they nod.

After an hour of dancing and with a glitter of perspiration on my skin, we are back at the bar to order another drink. Sammy giggles and slurs. "I can't believe you were actually going to kiss him. You weren't though - were you? I mean, you were just joking?"

Dante leans between us. "She can't do it. Her father would kill her."

"He'd ship her off to that convent he's always threatening her with." Bella laughs.

I stare across the bar at him.

Rufino is talking to another guy, a little closer to me than he was before, and I'm watching him again, wondering what would happen if I *did* just kiss him. It's not like the world would explode. He's just a guy.

"It was a stupid dare to begin with —" they are still discussing how I can't go through with it.

"None of you know what you're talking about. I *will do it.*" I say, undressing him in my mind, wondering if he would taste as good as he looks.

"Oh please, Bella was joking when she dared you. Even *you* aren't *that* crazy, Verity."

"Aren't I?" I grin.

"Oh my word, it's Verity, the attention whore."

I spin around to glare at the girl standing behind me. As soon as I set my eyes on Allie, I remember how much I hate her. She used to be my best friend. Many years ago. But my father kicked her father out of a business deal when he couldn't stick to the terms and she took it out on me by becoming a total bitch.

"Allie, don't push your luck with me tonight." I warn her, trying to keep my temper in check.

She turns towards my friends, addressing them. "Be careful. She's a backstabbing bitch. I would watch yourselves around her."

I don't know if it's the way she's tilting her head from side to side or that annoying high-pitched tone in her voice, but something inside me snaps and I leap towards her, throwing one hell of a punch.

My fist connects with her jaw and she squeals like a little pig, flying backwards, clutching at the people standing near her.

I should leave it at that - but I'm seething with rage - and drunk. So, I lean down and punch her again.

She kicks at me but misses.

Someone grabs me from behind and lifts me off her.

The bartender is yelling at me to calm down with his arm wrapped around my waist to hold me back.

"Get your hands off me." I demand, glaring at him. He steps away from me and holds his hands in the air. But he keeps his eyes fixed on me. "Let's not do this tonight."

I push my lips together. The bartender knows me because I come here often. But he also knows that I spend so much money here, I practically have shares in the place.

I sigh in annoyance. "I want her removed from this club. I never want to see her face in here again."

He sighs, but he waves a bouncer over and leans close to him to say something into his ear. The bouncer nods then scoops a crying Allie off the floor to carry her out of the club.

The bartender turns back to me. "It's done. But no more bullshit tonight, ok?"

I smile but continue to glare at him until he walks away, shaking his head.

"Holy fuck." Dante bursts out laughing. Bella and Sammy are wide eyed and then laughing too. I'm still way too pumped up with anger and adrenaline.

Fuck it.

I may as well go all in with the craziness.

I spin away from them - marching straight towards Rufino Vece.

My friends are shouting at me to come back, not to be stupid. It's too late, I have made up my mind.

Rufino's eyes are on me, dark and curious, as I step right into his personal space and, with no warning whatsoever, I grab the collar of his shirt, pull him down to my level and press my mouth against his.

As soon as our lips touch, my anger dissolves and I melt into him. His build is like that of a freaking Viking. Solid and broad and even taller than I thought. His muscles ripple beneath his shirt when he moves.

His hand travels up my spine, sending shivers through my entire body as he pulls me even closer against him.

Everything around me disappears and all I feel, and all I know, is him.

It's like a volcano has erupted and we are the energy that gets released from it. Time stops. His kiss is everything.

My heart is beating a million miles an hour when I finally step back.

He is staring at me with the calmest expression on his face.

I expected him to be furious, or at least taken aback, but he remains composed. Not saying a word.

I don't say a word either.

I got what I came for.

I did the dare.

I kissed the scary dangerous man, and nothing exploded.

Except me. I exploded a little.

Spinning away from him, I march all the way back to my friends and pick up the tequila they ordered for me and down it.

"What's the next dare?" I ask, grinning and throwing them *a don't mess with me* look.

I am empowered. Bold. crazy and like a total badass.

It's *freaking amazing.*

Everyone is staring at me in utter disbelief until Dante laughs.

"You *are* a psycho." He says, and everyone joins him in laughter.

"I need to dance." I tug Bella towards the dance floor and everyone else follows. My body is high. It's as though his lips were a drug, and it won't stop flooding me with adrenaline.

My heart won't stop beating like a wild horse's hooves running through an open plain, either.

My mind is still very much on the kiss and how he pushed up against me.

My eyes keep tracing back to where he's standing. I don't know what it is about him, but that calm aura seems to hide an undercurrent of extreme darkness. There is a secret in his eyes that I want to know more about.

My body is inexplicably tied to him now and I can't shake the feeling that the kiss was only the beginning of something bigger.

It can't be, though.

I'm just drunk, that's all.

I'm drunk and hyped up on tequila and I should just forget about the Vece. I did the dare. Move on.

Forcing myself to turn my back on him, I close my eyes and lift my hands in the air, letting the music soak through me and distract me from the way he causes my body to tingle.

I listen to the bass and let it pull me and push me until it's all I'm thinking about. The music can take me. It's all I need.

But that's when I feel his hands on me.

CHAPTER TWO
Rufino

She's been watching me all night like a fox with its eyes on its prey.

But I am nobody's prey. So, I stare back at her like a wolf, daring her to come closer.

I'm here to relax and have a few drinks. But she's distracting me. Not that I mind it. She's fucking gorgeous.

"Who is that?" I lean towards my acquaintance. He's someone I hang out with sometimes, but I can't call him a friend - I don't have friends. I prefer it that way. Friends are a risk I don't enjoy taking. Having friends requires trusting people and I don't trust anyone.

"That's Verity A'Vara. Fucking hot, but if you know what's good for you, don't even glance in her direction. She's nothing but trouble. She's literally hellfire." He shakes his head and rolls his shoulders back, shuddering at the thought of dealing with her.

I chuckle. She can't be *that* bad. She's just a girl.

"A'Vara." I mutter to myself. I know exactly who her father is. I did not know his daughter was that much of a minx, though. She stands out as the most beautiful woman I've ever seen.

Her bold attitude and that sassy smirk she keeps throwing in my direction only make me more curious about her.

Her wild blond hair hangs loose around her shoulders. Even from across the bar, I can see how blue her eyes are, complimented by the blue of her short, sexy dress.

She moves with confidence and sex appeal.

Another girl steps close to her and I can see Verity dislikes her. They exchange words and the tension between them explodes.

"Wooha." I chuckle when Verity flies forward and slams her fist into the other girl's face. She drops like a rock, landing hard on her ass.

"Told you. *Hellfire.*" My acquaintance pulls his mouth tight. "Fucking hellfire."

I watch, enthralled when Verity doesn't leave it at one punch but takes another swing at the girl. Whatever she said clearly pissed her off.

A bartender leaps over the bar and lifts Verity up in the air, but one look from her and he lets go, not willing to take her on himself. This girl has power, and she isn't afraid to use it.

In no time at all, her challenger is being carried out of the club and when Verity looks in my direction again, I'm struggling to hide the smile on my face.

I'm starting to like this girl.

Hellfire indeed.

My heart flick-flacks in my chest when starts walking towards me - she has something on her mind, but I have no idea what her intensions are.

Fuck, she is gorgeous. The closer she gets to me, the more obvious her beauty becomes. And that devilish shine in her eyes is sending an intense thrill through my body. I enjoy playing with fire, I always have.

She grabs my collar and pulls me down. I think she's going to punch me.

But out of nowhere, she kisses me.

For a second, I am stunned and frozen in place.

But very quickly, the electric current running between us sparks me back to life and I reach out to touch her, dragging her closer, running my hands over her body and the curve of her back.

My skin is on fire wherever my body is touching hers.

My senses are so heightened that I am drugged by her lips.

She steps back. My eyes are on her mouth. Plump, perfect pink lips.

She smirks at me and I hold her stare.

Then just as quickly as she arrived - she leaves.

Walking back to her friends as though I was nothing but a dare - something to conquer.

I lean my elbow against the bar counter and watch her.

What the fuck was that about?

Who the fuck does she think she's playing with?

I chuckle again, amused by the sheer audacity of it.

But I can't deny that she has my attention. She doesn't give a fuck at all, and I love that about her.

I watch her for a while, enjoying the way she moves on the dance floor and deciding how I want to handle this. But I know one thing for sure - I'm not done with her.

Verity A'Vara is not paying me any attention.

Although, despite her ignoring me, I can still feel the tension between us.

I push off from the bar and nod towards my acquaintance. "It was good to see you, Jim."

"You too, Red."

I make my way towards her.

When I step onto the dance floor, I wrap my hand around her waist from behind. I notice her friend's eyes are wide with shock or fear, as she takes a big step back and bumps into her other friend.

I enjoy having that effect on people. They should fear me.

Verity only glances over her shoulder and asks. "Can I help you with something, Vece?"

I grab her jaw, tilt her head back, and kiss her with much more force than she gave me. Pressing my hand against her stomach to hold her in place, I push my cock against her back.

She doesn't even flinch.

The kiss becomes more intense with each passing second. Her head tilted back, and her long neck exposed. I run my hand down her throat and wrap my fingers over it, squeezing ever so slightly.

I press my mouth close to her ear and whisper, "Come with me."

Without hesitation, to turns away from her friends and lets me take her hand.

"Verity - *no* - what the fuck are you *doing*?" one of them shouts.

She glances back at them and winks. It makes me laugh.

Fuck.

She's incredible.

She truly doesn't care. She's not afraid of anything. Hellfire.

Why do I see so much of myself in her?

Pushing through the crowd and letting her walk in my slipstream, I lead her off the dance floor and out of the club.

In the cool evening air outside, she takes a deep breath and giggles, grinning at me.

"Where are we going, Viking?" She asks.

"We're going to my place." I say, pulling the passenger door of my Mustang open, waiting for her to climb inside.

I close the door behind her and make my way around to the driver's side.

Neither of us says a word on the drive home, but I've got a dark grin spread across my face. Thinking about all the things I want to do with her.

She props her feet up on my dashboard, giving me the perfect view of her long, toned legs and those killer high heels.

I reach out and run my hand down the inside of her thigh.

She looks across at me, her lashes half lowered, giving her a demure look.

The garage door slides closed behind us and I turn the engine off.

The car door swings wide when I climb out, walking to her side and holding the door open.

She follows me into the house and as soon as the heavy wooden door closes behind us, I turn and pin her against the wall.

"You shouldn't go home with strangers." I growl, gliding my hands over her hips.

"Perhaps it's you that made a mistake by underestimating what I'm capable of. You shouldn't take strangers home." She replies, lifting her face towards mine, wrapping her hand around the back of my neck and kissing me. Her confidence is astounding. She lifts one leg, wrapping it against my hip as I run my hand along her thigh.

Every cell in my body fires at the same time.

Sharp electric spikes of need shoot through me as she rocks her body forward against mine.

My fingers drag her dress up over her hips and hook beneath her lace panties. I rip them off and she lets out a sharp gasp against my mouth. Her blue eyes looking darker.

Her gaze shoots a warning at me and she bites down on my lower lip, just enough to send a wild spark of adrenalin through me. My cock throbs as I lean into her. Letting her know what she is about to get.

Tugging my belt off, I slide it free and grab both of Verity's wrists in one hand, pinning them above her head against the wall.

Her eyes are tight on me while I wrap the leather belt around her wrists and bind her in place. Then

I pull my pants open, lift her up around my waist and thrust into her.

She groans as my cock spreads her open and fills her up, buried deep inside her.

She locks her legs tighter around my waist, hooking her tied wrists over my neck as I fuck her hard, slamming her body against the wall with each push.

With mounting intensity and heavy breathing, we move together. Her sweet moans ringing against my ear and her hair falling around her shoulders when she tilts her head back.

Every inch of my body is pulsing with carnal power.

I can't stop fucking her - going faster and faster - not even trying to slow down to make it last longer. I've lost all control.

Her cries get louder and louder with each penetration of my cock, causing her legs to shake and her hips to arch all the way forward.

She lets out a shaking gasp and her pussy tightens over my cock. Her muscles wave and pulse when her orgasm rushes through her.

A second later, and my cock is rigid inside her, explosive and aggressive. Ecstasy floods out of me.

She slides down the wall as I loosen my grip on her. She's staring at me with a cheeky grin on her face.

"I'm going to grab an Uber. Thanks for a fun time." She says, pulling her dress down over her hips, swaying a little and then giggling at herself.

I chuckle and grab her arm to steady her.

"You aren't going anywhere, little vixen. I'm not done with you."

"Oh. Well, who says I'm not done with you?"

I shake my head. "Is everything with you a challenge?" I growl, lifting Verity and throwing her over my shoulder to carry her upstairs to my bedroom.

I toss her onto my bed and stand looking down at her while I get undressed.

She grins, rolls onto her stomach, and moves so that she is on all fours with her ass pointed right at me. And of course - she's not wearing any panties because I tore those from her body.

My cock is hard again.

She giggles and sits up on her knees to take her dress off and throw it at me. Then she looks over her shoulder at me with a smirk.

I climb onto the bed and push her back down onto her stomach, shoving her hard against the mattress. I spread her legs wide with my legs and plunge my cock into her from behind.

Her screams get muffled against the pillow as her face is pushed into it. I fuck her hard, grunting every time I thrust forward.

I hear her giggle and take it as a challenge. Threading my fingers through her hair, I pull hard, arching her back and pulling her head towards me.

She is gasping and moaning and loving the games we're playing.

And I can't fucking get enough of her.

I don't know what time we pass out, tangled in each other - exhausted and satisfied.

I can smell her hair spread out over my pillow and my chest.

She smells like dark strawberries and magnolia.

When I fall asleep, I dream of chasing her through the woods while she runs, always head of me, just out of reach, laughing at that mischievous little giggle of hers.

CHAPTER THREE
Verity

The blissful unawareness of sleep drifts away from me as my body wakes up.

At first I don't know where I am. The room is unfamiliar, the bedding is dark grey, something smells like musk and pine. A rich, dark scent that makes my skin tingle.

My cheek is resting on a very solid, very muscular chest and the sun is right on my face, too bright.

Far too bright.

Blinking away the glaring pain behind my eyeballs, I push my memory around until it wakes up and registers where I am and what happened last night.

Oh no.

That's not good at all.

I should not have done that.

Of all the stupid ideas I've ever come up with, this one has to be top of the list.

Rufino *Vece*. What the hell was I thinking?

If my father ever finds out…

I don't even want to think about it. This is too much - I need to go. Should go right now. Before he even wakes up.

Whatever, who am I kidding? I don't even care. I love causing shit. I love doing stupid things. This particular stupid thing is way up on my list of achievements, but I don't give a damn what anyone thinks.

Glancing at my phone, I see a ton of messages from my friends.

Scrolling through them, I get the gist of their panic, amusement, and desperate need for an update. I chuckle to myself and immediately regret it.

My head is pounding like a steady drum beat. Thump. Thump. Thump.

I groan loudly, reaching my hand up to massage the headache out of my skull, but it's locked inside there.

Fuck.

I drank way too much last night. *Again.*

But at least I remember everything. I'm not one of those people that forget or have to find out from their friends what happened afterwards. I always remember everything.

Even though I might have preferred to pretend like I don't remember this specific thing.

I can't believe I slept with Rufino Vece. The Viking of a man I am now sprawled across.

Mm. It was fun, though. Like the fun where you are pushing boundaries, but that's what makes it ten times better. And damn - he played my body like a musical instrument. The things he did to me.

No, wait, I can't get carried about remembering all of that. I need to get up.

Lifting my head, I glance over his rugged face. The square jaw patterned with a dark beard, short and neat - fire red.

No wonder people call him Red.

I think he looks like a Viking.

And I have a thing for Viking looking men.

This one fits every single one of my boxes when it comes to looks.

Damn - he is gorgeous.

But also dangerous, my family's enemy and someone I should *not be waking up in bed next to.*

I roll off him with a huff, tugging at the sheet that is over both of us and wrapping it around my body, not caring that I climb off the bed and walk away, leaving him with nothing covering him. Besides, it gives me a chance to steal another look at him.

If I wasn't staring at the fucking hot, sculpted body of Rufino Vece, I would climb right back into bed with him. But I can't be stupid enough to make that same mistake twice. And this time I won't even be able to blame it on the alcohol.

Turning away from him, ignoring the heightened buzz I get when I look at him too long, I make my way to the kitchen.

Now that I am not distracted by his hulking sex appeal, coffee is all I care about.

I bang around his kitchen, finding the cabinet with the coffee mugs and whatever else I need.

I make the most perfect cup of coffee and then lean against the kitchen counter to take my first sip. The first sip is always the best.

Hot, creamy liquid flows down my throat, soaking up the pain of my hangover and for a second I feel like I'm going to survive the day.

I sigh with satisfaction and close my eyes to enjoy it.

"Wonderful coffee?" His voice forces me to open my eyes and glare at him.

"It *was really* great coffee when I could enjoy it in *silence*." I chirp.

He laughs, pulling a mug out for himself.

"How are you feeling?"

I sigh. I must make sure he understands that last night was just a mistake. A dumbass, drunk decision I need to forget about.

I scrunch my nose, wondering if I can forget his solid body presses up against mine.

I have to.

"Listen, last night was fun and all, but I'm going to head out now."

"In my sheet?" his eyes trace over my body. I pull my mouth to the side and narrow my eyes towards him.

I thought he would be reluctant to see me go - not worried about his sheet.

"Mmph." I huff, rolling my eyes.

What is it about this man that I like so much?

He's got this calm, *I don't give a fuck* attitude. I think I see a lot of myself in him. That similar disregard and the same defiant, yet adventurous streak.

I need to leave. Now.

Like right fucking now.

I can't be standing here eyeing him up and down, wondering about the things I am wondering about.

Rufino Vece is off limits.

I walk out of the kitchen back into the bedroom and slip my dress on over my head, leaving the sheet crumpled on the bed.

Then I pick up my coffee mug and my phone, calling an Uber.

Three minutes wait. Not bad at all.

My feet ache a little when I slip them back into the heels. I guess I danced more than usual last night.

Carrying the coffee, I head back to the kitchen.

My eyes trace over his body again.

No shirt.

Grey sweatpants.

His broad shoulders patterned with the curve and flex of well-defined muscles.

He's looking fucking divine. And he looks hungry when he gazes at my body.

"Have a cool day." I shrug. "My Uber is here."

"Leaving already? Don't you want breakfast or something? My driver can take you home later." He lifts his coffee to his lips and takes a slow sip.

"Nope, I'm done here."

He narrows his eyes, trying to figure me out. But no one can ever figure *me* out, so good luck with that. I prefer to keep people on their toes, guessing about what's coming next. Most of the time, I don't even know what I'm going to do next. I find it's best to decide in the moment and go with the flow.

Life is more fun that way - instead of bending to other people's rules and expectations.

I grin, feeling cheeky.

"Bye." I say and turn to walk out of the front door, sipping my coffee as I go.

"That's my mug," He says, sounding confused.

"Is it? I don't see your name on it." I smirk, pushing the door open and walking out of his house, towards where the Uber is waiting for me on the street.

"Lexington Building on Seventh Street." The Uber smells of dash polish as though he's just had it cleaned.

"Yes, miss." He confirms the address, and heading towards my father's building.

My father likes to keep his eyes on the city. Instead of buying a mansion out somewhere away from the city center, he bought a building and converted the top two floors into our home.

I'm fine with it.

I like to keep my eyes on the city too.

Living somewhere in the suburbs would bore me out of my mind.

I keep drinking my coffee while the driver keeps throwing me a random glance in the rearview mirror.

"Can I help you with something?" I say in a sarcastic tone.

He turns his eyes back to the road and doesn't look again.

Scrolling through the ton of messages I've received, I tell my friends that they can get all the updates when I see them. I'm not sure what to tell them.

I can't believe it happened.

I went through with the dare and for some stupid reason took it even further than that and go home with the guy.

The worst part, the part I am trying to ignore or deny or just not believe - is that I want to see him again. Yeah, stupid. I know.

But why wouldn't I want the one thing I'm not supposed to have and the sex - I can't describe how good it was.

It was so intense with him, my heart was racing, and my body was on fire against his.

I've never felt that with anyone before.

And there's something else.

Something that makes me want to roll my eyes at myself because it sounds so cliche.

I feel like I know him. Like my soul knows him.

When I let the thought take form in my head, I roll my eyes at myself.

Yip.

Ridiculous

The Uber driver stops outside the building and I head inside. The private elevator only goes to the top floor. There is another one on the other side of the building for anyone wanting to access anything other than the top two.

It's a long ride up.

I hope my father isn't home. I'm not in the mood for another one of his lectures.

Unfortunately, luck is not on my side.

"Where have you been? Why didn't you answer my messages?" he demands as soon as I walk through the door.

"I stayed at Sammy's place." I smile. "Morning, daddy."

"Like hell you did. Where the fuck were you? His fury clear as the veins on his forehead protrude. Which means they pretty much always stand out.

"Daddy, stop being such a worrier. I was at Sammy's."

"Stop doing this, Verity. You can't be out all night and sneaking home in the same dress you went clubbing in. When are you going to grow up? I can still smell the alcohol on you. People see you. People I know and work with. What do you think they say about your behavior?"

I sigh, grin and roll my eyes.

"Stop being so dramatic. And I'm not *sneaking* home." I laugh, ignoring his obvious annoyance.

"Verity, I need you to take this seriously? Don't make me send you away. Start learning to behave like a lady."

He's always threatening to send me to a convent in Europe, but I don't believe him. Even if I thought the threat was real, it wouldn't change who I am - I don't *want* to be a lady. I want to have *fun*.

"I'm going to shower." I call as I walk up the stairs towards my bedroom.

"Verity - I'm talking to you—"

His voice fades when I close my bedroom door.

I'm twenty-three. I'm not a kid anymore but he still tries to control everything. It drives me crazy.

After a shower and a fresh new outfit I'm almost human again. But if I really want to get rid of this hangover, I need to get some food in my body.

Picking up my phone to see if anyone is free for breakfast I scroll through my messages and my heart stops.

> Unknown: You left in far too much of a hurry. I want more.

Of course, I know exactly who it is. But how did he get this number? No one gets this number unless I give it to them.

> Me: Who says that what you want matters?

I giggle when I hit send.

Why do I feel like a girl with her first crush?

I can't let this guy get to me in this way.

I'd better be careful.

> Rufino: What I want matters because I always get what I want.

> Me: Prove it.

If he wants to see me again, he's going to work for it. I won't make it easy, just because it's more fun that way.

Besides, I can't let him know I want to see him just as much.

CHAPTER FOUR
Rufino

Verity left my penthouse with my coffee mug.

The audacity of it makes me want her a hundred times more. I chuckle every time I think about it.

She's so fucking cocky and full of shit.

Everything about her is a challenge. She's feisty, rude and carefree in a such a way that I can't stop thinking about her. It's driving me crazy.

Finding her number was easy. I have access to a lot of information that is not public knowledge. It comes at a price, but this price was worth every cent I paid.

We've been flirting over messages all day.

It hasn't even been twenty-four hours since I last saw her, and I want to see her again as soon as possible.

Sitting in the meeting at work I'm busy talking to her on my phone.

"Rufino, are we interrupting something?" Masaccio says with annoyance.

I look up from the message I was reading.

"Not at all, please, carry on."

He snarls. The topic of conversation is a new shipment, and he's stressed about it. I couldn't give less of a fuck if I tried. My brothers are assholes. They have been assholes my entire life - making it too fucking clear that I am an outsider in their group. My red hair and imposing height setting me apart from them - making me different. They decided when I was young that I was adopted and have spent their lives making sure I understood I wasn't one of them.

The nicknames they made up for me where endless. Devil kid. Fire brains. Carrot. The gingerbread man. Lighthouse.

But the one that stuck was Red.

It stuck because I let it stick.

I would become aggressive to the point where two of my brothers had to go to the hospital on separate occasions.

It got so bad when I was around thirteen years old that my father had me DNA tested. He knew what the results would be, but he wanted to make it clear to my brothers.

I *am* their brother.

There is no question about it.

Yet, they *still* continued to remind me I was not part of their inner circle.

So - fuck them.

Fuck their family meetings and their loyalty to each other.

Absolutely, I stand by my family no matter what. I would not cross that line, but I don't have to hang out with them or be part of their shit.

I have better things to do with my time.

Typing out my reply to Verity I am back to ignoring Masaccio.

> Me: So, when can I see you? I need to get my coffee mug back. It's my favorite one.

> Verity: This coffee mug is my hostage now. It's going to cost you if you want it back. We will need to open negotiations.

I grin. This girl has caught my attention. I will play her games, and I will win.

> Me: Name the price. Anything you want.

> Verity: I'll have to think about it. But in the meantime I might be at Collision tomorrow night.

> Me: I might be there too. What a coincidence.

I guess I'm going to Collision tomorrow night then.

When we finished up chatting I email the club manager at Collision and book a VIP table in the private area. I want to spend some time alone with her. Out of the watchful eye of the public.

The little time we spent near each other last time was a risk. We need to be careful if we are going to play with fire.

But I want to play with fire.

Us being seen together could literally start a war between our families. The relationship between my brothers and the A'Vara's has always been sketchy - on the brink of something violent. I'm pretty sure her father would want to tear me apart if he found out I spent a night with his daughter.

I reckon he'd want blood if he found out I was doing nothing more than speaking to her.

♥

Collision is full, wall to wall people, and the music is vibrating against my skin as I stand on the balcony of the VIP section with my eyes scanning across the club for her.

I'm filled with nervous tension. The thick thrumming energy of anticipation that I can't shake. It's strange to me to feel this way about a girl.

Something about her has infected my mind and body.

Every moment of every day she is there in my thoughts.

And I'm fine with it.

Verity walks into the club looking like a goddess, dragging my attention onto her to the point where I cannot look anywhere else.

Her black, short dress dips low in the front, almost to her belly button, showing off the carved line down the center of her toned stomach.

A groove from below her breasts that travels between her ribs - I want to trace my tongue over it. All the way down to taste her again.

She glances up at me as though she can sense me.

Our eyes meet and one corner of her mouth curls up into a mischievous grin.

She is here alone.

That's what I wanted.

However, when she makes her way through the crowd, many people greet her. She is well known here, just like I am. We have to be so careful.

"Hello, Viking." She smiles, her eyes tracing over my body with suggestion while she bites her lower lip. She steps forward and brushes her cheek against mine. Not the greeting I've been waiting for.

I slip my hand around her narrow waist and tug her tight against my body.

Pressing my lips against her mouth I kiss her, her hot breath against my skin. My entire body sparks.

My cock stirs and I wonder how I will make it through the night without fucking her on the couch in our private booth.

Perhaps I won't.

Perhaps that is exactly what I'll do.

There is a first time for everything.

"Champagne?" I ask when I step away, taking her hand and looking down at her. Those bright blue eyes teasing me with secrets I want to learn. I want to know everything about her. I want to read her like an open book.

She nods, a soft smile on her rose lips.

The VIP room I've booked is a lot more secluded than the main VIP balcony. I lead her to it and pull the heavy velvet curtain closed behind us.

Below us, on the dance floor, crowds of people move in time to the same beat, like waves on the ocean, all flowing in the same direction. I watch them for a second, but they can't hold my attention. I turn back to her. She drops her clutch onto the table next to the silver ice bucket.

"Excellent choice." She comments, lifting the champagne to look at the label.

"I only make the best choices." I say, my eyes on her as I pull her towards me.

She stands with her hands on my chest, tracing her fingers over my pecs.

The top of her head almost reaches my shoulders.

I could break her like a twig, but something suggests she is covered in thorns.

Verity bites her lip and throws me a look that sends hot shivers down my spine.

"I was hoping you were more inclined towards

making bad choices." Her eyes narrow with a silent challenge.

On her tip toes she wraps her fingers around the back of my neck and pulls me towards her for another kiss. Our lips touch and nothing else matters. The world around me disappears and all I feel or see is her.

She blocks off the chaos of my thoughts and silences my mind.

This girl might just be the death of me, and I'm not even bothered if that turns out to be the case.

She joins me on the sofa, while I pour us each a glass of champagne.

The thing that takes me more by surprise than anything else is how well we get on when we are just talking. Yes, the sharp electric current between us is a constant. Rich sensual tension that sparks beneath my fingertips when I brush them over her. But apart from that - we share the same dark sense of humor, that same streak of cheeky arrogance and a talent for the game of teasing.

She doesn't want to be tamed - neither do I. But

the thought of making her submissive to *me* is driving me wild.

After a bottle of champagne the risks we take are escalating.

"Where is your security guard?" I ask as she climbs onto my lap, straddling her legs over my thighs and grabbing my face in her hands.

"Don't worry about them. They made the mistake of tracking my phone." She grins.

"And where is your phone, Verity?"

"It's gone for a little drive with a friend of mine."

She brushes her thumb across my lips, pulling my mouth open and then wrapping her own lips over mine.

I can't help the growl that rumbles through my chest when she rocks her hips over me. My cock growing harder by the second.

I grab her waist and push her harder against me.

The little gasp that falls from her lips is my undoing.

I reach behind her, my hands wrapping around her ass, letting my fingers trace between her ass cheeks. She isn't wearing underwear. She is asking for this. I dip my finger inside her pussy and her breath catches.

She locks her eyes into mine.

Pulling my zip open I free my cock and she doesn't break eye contact when I push myself inside her.

This is way too risky.

This is beyond stupid.

But I can't fucking stop.

Her nails dig through my shirt into my shoulder and I push her back and forth on my cock.

I can see the dance floor over the edge of our balcony, moving and flowing and flooded with people.

But none of them can see us.

And if they could, all they would see are two people making out on a sofa.

That's what I tell myself as I thrust up into her and let the blissful blur of champagne continue to taint my better judgement.

Verity is moaning against my ear and it's so fucking hard to control myself.

I want to rip her dress off her body and wrap my lips over her nipples. I want to grab her thighs and spread them open so that I can fuck her deeper.

We move together, both striving for that same control.

But even without the freedom of movement I would prefer, I am so close to exploding and I can feel how her pussy is pulsing over my cock.

Her nails dig in deeper and her legs shake.

She grinds herself against me and bites her lower lips.

In the dim light of the club, with red and pink lights flashing around us, she tilts her head back and gasps when the orgasm locks her onto me.

My cock goes rigid inside her.

The release is pure ecstasy as I come more intensely than I thought possible.

She giggles but doesn't climb off my lap in a hurry.

Instead she leans over and picks up her champagne, sipping it, whilst watching my face.

"I think you're bad for me." She whispers against my ear.

"Why is that?" I chuckle.

"Because - with you - there seem to be no limits."

"There aren't any limits, little vixen. And even if there were - you and I can break them all."

CHAPTER FIVE
Verity

My phone slides into the back pocket of my jeans. I'm ready to go.

Two security guards dressed in fitted black suites are standing close by in the living room of my father's penthouse.

I pull my mouth to the side in annoyance, shooting a glare at both of them.

"I really don't need them today. I'm just going to meet Sammy and Bella for some lunch."

My father huffs in annoyance. "Verity, you know the rules. They go everywhere you go. Why do you have to push me every time?" he snarls angrily.

I bite my lip. The more I argue the more difficult it will make for me to lose them later. But if I don't argue at all, he might be just as suspicious.

It's getting harder every time I try to elude them because they are learning all my tricks.

Sighing to get my point across I spin on my heels, my high-top sneakers squeaking on the marble floor of the penthouse.

"Keep your phone on you, Verity." My father warns me without looking up from the newspaper he's reading.

The security guards both follow me out of the living room and into the private elevator.

"Where are we going this afternoon, Miss A'Vara?" one of them asks. I can't even be bothered to learn their names. They come and go so frequently. These guys are already in trouble for losing me when I went to Collision last week, and I've evaded them once more since then - two days ago when I met Rufino for a cocktail at the yacht club - which is where I plan to go now.

These guards are already on the shit list with my father and I know that if I slip away from them one or two more times, they will lose their jobs and be replaced by new men with new names that I also won't bother to learn.

"I'm going to meet my friend at the mall. We want to do some shopping, have lunch and then maybe a cocktail afterward at the Pink Flamingo on main street." I glare at him, daring him to challenge me.

"Mm." He huffs, his eyes tight on me. He's cute. But he doesn't come close to Rufino. No one does.

Fuck, that Viking is gorgeous.

I shouldn't be so attracted to *one* man. Getting hooked on one guy leads to a relationship and I don't want a relationship. The commitment, the promises, the boring monotony. That isn't for me.

Next thing I'll be married, knocked-up, and locked in for life. Some trophy wife that her husband tries to control.

Fuck that.

But Rufino is making me question myself. My wants. My desires.

I'm not supposed to think about him all day and miss him when I'm not with him.

It's not what I do. But he's got me hooked.

I keep reassuring myself that it's just a physical thing. Some crazy sexual attraction that'll I'll soon get bored with, but somehow I know I'm lying to myself.

I smile as the elevator carries us down to the parking garage.

"I'll take my car, you can follow." I say, pressing the button on my keys and hearing my car bleep in the underground cavern.

"No, that is not an option." One man says, climbing into my passenger seat.

"I'm pretty sure I pay you, so you have to do what I say." I snap in annoyance.

"Your father pays me. I do what he says." He replies blandly.

The other guys climb into the second car to follow us.

"Whatever." I sigh, starting the engine and revving.

My tires scream against the concrete flooring when I take off at a reckless speed, heading out into the street and towards the mall where I already have a plan to ditch these two assholes and make another escape.

"Worked just the way I wanted it too." I laugh to myself as I climb into the cab and tell him to take me to the yacht club.

Those fucking idiots are going to be furious when they realize the changing room in that shop has two exits.

Red is sitting at a table in the far corner, his back to the wall and his eyes on the door when I walk through it.

I love how subtle his smile is. And it belongs to me. His lips curl up at the corners, pressing dimples into his cheeks while his eyes drink me in.

"You got away faster this time." He laughs.

"Those two will not have a job by the end of the week."

Before I sit down I pull my phone out of my back pocket and put it on the table.

"Isn't that risky?" he knots his brows.

"No, I called the guys you suggested. He installed that program for me and now I can set my location for the tracker. So they are going to be following me around the mall for the next few hours, wondering why the hell I'm always two steps ahead of them."

When he laughs, it's like warm caramel running over my skin.

My heart flips and tightens in my chest.

These are not things I am used to.

I swallow hard, telling my heart to be quiet, but when my eyes lock with his - those pale green pools of mystery and untold stories - it's my mind that goes silent and my heart that beats even louder.

I look away, picking up the menu to distract myself.

What is going on with me?

This isn't normal.

I bite my lip browsing over the menu but not reading it at all.

"I've ordered you a blue gin with mint and strawberry." He is still watching me.

"You remembered." I set the menu down and tilt my head to the side as I narrow my gaze over him.

He says nothing.

He doesn't need to say anything for me to know what he's thinking.

Beneath the table he reaches out and grabs the edge of my chair, dragging it around to be next to his.

His hand sends shockwaves of pleasure through me when he wraps it around my thigh.

"I've missed you." He whispers, his breath hot against my cheek.

I lean towards him, goosebumps covering my body.

"I can't stop thinking about—" I bite my words back. Telling him that is not the best way to play hard to get. Am I even trying to play at this point?

He makes me feel like every man I've ever looked at is just a boy compared to him. None of them could keep up with me. None of them challenged me or sparked this fire in me. He is the gasoline, and I am the match.

"I can't stop thinking about you either." He chuckles, picking up on my hesitation.

"I was *going* to say that I can't stop thinking about the amazing salmon they serve here. I have no idea what *you* are talking about." I smirk.

"Mm. The salmon. Of course." That half smile. Those deep dimples.

Fuck, he is fucking divine.

The afternoon sun blinks over the salty water of the yacht club and up against the crisp white and blue boats tied to their docks.

We talk. We joke. We share stories.

It's as though we never run out of things to say to each other.

Laughter rolls off my lips and my heart slips a little deeper into him as the afternoon drifts on in a lazy stream of gin and food.

The more I get to know him the more I worry

about where I am going to end up if I keep this up. I can't stay away. I don't want to either.

He is the gamble I should *not* take - but the most delicious one I have ever tasted.

The alluring danger of this man, the fun enticement, and the risk I take every time the thought of him flickers through my body - it's going to get me sent to a convent in Europe.

♥

Day after day I meet him.

Sometimes it's only for a moment. Five minutes together where he will push me up against a wall in the bathroom at the mall, or a restaurant or in the parking lot.

Sometimes I get away from a few hours and we can talk and spend real time together, but the fact is that every time it happens the danger increases, and my father is becoming more and more suspicious of what I'm up to. They have assigned me a new set of personal security guards who are more intense than ever before.

The more I have to keep my distance from him the more I want him.

His body haunts my dreams at night, and I wake up thinking of his eyes on me and his hands against my skin.

This afternoon Sammy, Bella and I are shopping, and I've told Rufino to meet me here. The girls and I are sitting at a small coffee shop in the mall, my security guards are close by their eyes on me at all times.

I spot Rufino in the distance and smile.

"What secret joke aren't you sharing?" Bella asks, sipping her coffee.

"Nothing. I need to pee though. I'll be right back." I stand up, Rufino's eyes are on me as I make my way to the side, down a narrow passage and into the ladies room.

With my heart racing I wait, my back against the wall near the corner, trying to choose a spot where I can watch from both directions to make sure my security doesn't follow me here.

When Rufino's deep voice calls out to me I jump, tense with anticipation.

Turning towards him I leap into his arms.

He grins then kisses me, his lips hot against mine.

"I'm so tired of all these brief encounters. I want to see you again." I whine, annoyed about how efficient these new security guards are.

He looks down at me, brushing a long curl of hair from my face and tucking it behind my ear. "I know, my angel. But you know the risks. What about the club?"

"Collision? The VIP section?" I grin and a thrill of desire pulses through my entire body.

He nods, his pupils dilating at the memory of us on the sofa.

"I can meet you there on Saturday." My heart races.

"Miss A'Vara?" A voice calls out to me.

"Fuck. It's my security. You have to go." I whisper.

"Saturday." He confirms, then kisses me hard, pushing me against the wall and causing my body to ignite.

When I open my eyes Rufino is walking away from me.

One of the new security men steps around the corner into the passageway outside the bathrooms.

I clear my throat and walk past him, back into the coffee shop, ignoring his questioning glare as I make my way back towards my friends.

"You seem to be in a great mood." Sammy notices when I sit down.

"I am. Hey, what did you guys think of that white sequin dress we saw earlier? I think I want to go back and get it after lunch."

"It was beautiful. You can wear it to the party this weekend."

"What party?"

Sammy rolls her eyes. "Don't you read your messages anymore?" She sighs. "The Star Lounge - I've booked us a private booth."

"Oh, of course." I giggle. "I just forgot for a second."

I won't be going to the Star Lounge though. I have a more enticing invite.

Sammy and Bella are going to be annoyed again when I make some lame excuse on the night, but they'll get over it.

The only person I actually want to spend any time with at the moment is him.

CHAPTER SIX
Rufino

Walking into the warehouse I'm already tense and annoyed.

It's late.

It's Saturday.

And I don't see any reason to be calling a meeting now.

Tuomo sounded arrogant on the phone when he called earlier, and I think that him and Masaccio have it in for me this evening.

My brothers are all seated when I step through the office door into the boardroom section. Our regular meeting area.

"You're late." Masaccio snarls.

I don't bother replying.

I am late.

But who the fuck cares?

These meetings are a waste of time. They could just email me the key points afterwards instead of making me sit through hours of bullshit planning.

Everyone's eyes are glued to me as I walk around the table to take a seat at the spot next to Celso.

He nods, a silent greeting.

I nod back. Celso is the one I have the least issues with.

I guess it's because he doesn't share the same mother as the rest of us and he was taunted almost as much as I was growing up - outcast from the group in his own way.

However, being the youngest of all of us he got away with everything.

Our father has a soft spot for him so despite the taunting he endured from Masaccio and Tuomo he didn't struggle as much as I did.

"We need to discuss how the fuck we are going to make up for the lost profits on that fuck up of a shipment two days ago." Masaccio is looking down at some paperwork, addressing all of us. "Does anyone have any ideas regarding how we can go about getting a new shipment to the client, but not lose profit?"

Tuomo is about to speak, but I end up interrupting him.

"What shipment?" I ask, not knowing there was an issue with any of the past weeks deliveries.

The way Masaccio pulls his mouth I can see he wanted me to ask this question. He baited me into it.

He shakes his head with his mouth tight and his eyes narrowed.

"Are you fucking kidding me, Red?" he shouts, slamming the paperwork against the table. "Maybe if you bothered to stay in touch or come to the warehouse more often, you would know what the fuck was going on in the *family* business. You are *never* around. You think you can—"

"I do *whatever* is required of me." I snarl at him, my defenses high and my hackles rising.

"Yeah - you do whatever is required and not a fucking drop more. That's the problem though isn't it. You don't give a shit about putting in any effort over whatever the bare-minimum that is required of you."

"Why the fuck would I? What did you assholes ever do for me?"

"We're your fucking family." Masaccio yells.

"Oh - *now* you want to pretend I'm part of the team. Now when you *need* something from me? I work fucking hard for this family. Don't you dare question my loyalty to it?"

"What the fuck is wrong with you, Red? You're acting like you don't want to be here." Tuomo sighs.

Because I don't.

But I know better than to say that out loud.

As much as I will fight with my brothers I have learned over the years what the limits are. What pushing it too far looks like and what the consequences of that are. I hold back only for the sake of saving myself the annoyance and trouble of dealing with the backlash and their bloated egos.

I lean back in my chair with my arms folded across my chest.

I am clenching my jaw to stop myself from speaking that it's starting to ache.

"Whatever. Let's carry on." Celso says, waving his hand in the air and gesturing towards Masaccio.

Masaccio continues to glare at me.

"You need to get your shit together, Red. I don't know what the hell is going on with you, but your absence has been noted and the lack of effort won't go ignored for much longer."

"I've got better things to do with my time." I snap, standing up and sending the chair skidding out from behind me.

Turning towards the door I ignore Tuomo's heavy sigh and Celso telling me to sit down and let it go.

Fuck all of them.

I do *not* have to deal with this shit.

I do my job, I put the effort in. I just do it, on my own, without them hovering over my shoulder and trying to control every move I make. Masaccio isn't my fucking boss. Not until our father hands him the reigns to the empire.

"This meeting is important." Mas growls.

"Email me the key points." I dismiss him and walk out of the meeting room.

My heart is pounding as adrenaline courses though me.

This was a complete waste of my time and all it's done is to irritate me even more.

Climbing into my car I sit in the driver's seat for a minute, trying to push the agitation out of my body - but it's not working.

I roll my neck in a circle, flex my shoulders, and start the engine.

I have a little vixen to meet at a club in town.

That's where I want to be.

She is the only one who has and deserves my attention.

Gravel spits out behind my car as a wheel spin away from the warehouse.

They messed up that shipment - they can figure out how to fix it.

When I get to the club Verity is already there, waiting for me at the bar.

I walk towards her, grab her in my arms and kiss her.

She tenses and pushes me away. Tilting her head she looks amused and curious.

"What the hell are you doing? My security guards are down here somewhere watching."

"Then let's go up to VIP. Let them sit with the commoners and wait."

I grab her hand and pull her along with me. She laughs, shaking her head.

"Someone put you in a foul mood."

In our private area, with the heavy velvet curtain pulled closed, I drag her towards me again. "I'm tired of sneaking around. I want you. Let's go away for a weekend together."

Somewhere in the back of my mind I know it's not possible. It would stir up chaos if we were caught - but at this moment, I don't even want to think about anyone else opinion and driven by a fiery desire to be with her.

I am tired of waiting. I'm tired of not just being able to have her anytime, anywhere, *all the time.*

"You're really sexy when you're angry." She whispers seductively, running her fingertips over my jaw.

I slide my hands down her back, over her ass, and then lift her in my arms - wrapping her legs around my waist.

Her laughter turns into a sharp gasp when I grab a handful of her silky, long hair and yank her head back so that I can kiss the curve of her neck.

Every cell in my body is electrified.

My cock is so hard it's aching as it pushes against my pants.

I know what I need.

And I don't give a fuck about risk right now.

I push Verity's back against the wall, still holding her in my arms.

Tugging my pants open she squeals as I rip her panties to the side and shove my cock into her pussy.

Her body shudders with pleasure and her words come out in a struggle between heavy breaths. "They'll - they'll see - us." She moans as I fuck her against the wall.

"Let them watch." I growl against her hair, not willing to stop.

Her nails scratch down the back of my neck, leaving red raw lines on my skin.

I can't stop and *she* isn't even asking me to.

My cock plunges into her, over and over again, thrusting hard and moving fast. She cries out louder, not bothering to hide the sound of her pleasure - it's all lost in the heavy beat of music, anyway. No one can hear us up here.

Between the intensity of my outburst, the danger of what we're doing and our fierce connection - she is already close to coming all over me. I can feel it. I can see it in her eyes.

I push harder, grabbing her around the throat and squeezing just enough to make her lips part.

Gasping, she tightens her pussy over my cock, then closes her eyes and loses herself in the orgasm that waves through her.

I slam into her again, her body jolting against the wall behind her.

A deep growl thunders through me when I explode into her.

When it's over I step away, letting her feet slide to the floor.

She is grinning a wicked, delightful smile.

"I think people should piss you off more often." She teases me.

Grabbing her face in my hand I press my mouth over hers.

"I think we should run away together and escape this bullshit city."

She walks away from me, towards the bottle of vodka waiting on the table.

Pouring us each a shot she lifts her in the air.

"Who knows what the future holds?" Verity bites her lip, narrows her eyes and then throws her head back to take the shot.

I stare at her for a moment, wondering if anything rattles her. Wondering if anything I do would push her too far - past the point of risk she will take. So far she has proven herself to be just as adventurous as I am. Just as wild and fired up and dangerous.

In my eyes we there is no more perfect person we are made for each other.

In my mind I've already decided that we are going to be together. All I need to do is figure out a way to make that happen.

By hell or high water I will make her mine. I'm not willing to let her slip through my fingers.

"Do you want another one?" She asks, already pouring it.

I step behind her, wrapping my arms around her waist and pulling her back against my chest. "Run away with me, little vixen. I'm serious."

She sighs and shakes her head. "My father would kill us both."

"If it wasn't for your father - would you want to be with me?"

She turns in my arms, looking up at me with a trace of confusion on those beautiful blue eyes.

"Do you mean - like a proper relationship? Something serious?"

I chuckle. "I'm asking you if you like me - or if this is just a fun thing on the side for you?"

"Mm." She says, a sly grin on her lips. "Do you like me? Would you want to be in a relationship with me?"

I take her jaw in my hand and lock my gaze with hers. "Let me put it this way - if another man ever touches you I will tear him to pieces and leave him scattered across the city for others to see as a warning."

She giggles.

A sound that ripples through me like a silver bullet.

"Yes, I'd date you." She says and not committal. Always keeping me on my toes.

I love the fact that I can't work her out. I love the way she makes me work to understand her and how she makes me chase her.

It's the hunt.

It's been the hunt since the moment I first saw her.

CHAPTER SEVEN
Verity

Red's eyes are so piercing I'm struggling to keep my usually easy, cool, and casual attitude in check. My heart is racing when he asks me if I want to be with him.

I do.

But the thought also terrifies me. The idea of any type of commitment. It's so - serious. So final. But it doesn't have to be. I just can go with the flow and see where it takes me.

I want Rufino to take me - wherever he goes. Whatever he does.

I want to be with him.

And yes, that terrifies me.

Needing someone was not on my to do list today.

But if I am going to be with anyone - it's him. He lets me be myself. He never says no to what I want, and he is as wild and chaotic as I am.

In fact, he drives my wildness and pushes my boundaries in the best ways.

He's perfect.

And I *would* date him.

But it's not possible. My father would never let it happen. So, I can fantasize about these things from a safe distance, but I could never date Rufino.

I stare at him through lowered lashes, wondering why he's asking these things. But I'm glad he did because I've been wanting the answers too. I don't mind playing games - as long as I know it's a game. my heart has been slipping, tripping over him, falling for him - and if that's happening to me while he's still thinking this is just a game - well that would be a recipe for disaster.

The most mischievous smile dances over my face.

He tilts his head.

"What is it?" his deep voice melts me every time he speaks.

I lick my lips. If I ask this question, there is no going back.

But fuck it. Since when did I hold back with whatever was on my mind.

"Are you in love with me, Rufino Vece?" I stare at him. Not letting my emotions show.

He remains silent, those pale green eyes looking right into my soul.

I feel the anxiety growing in my stomach.

I was stupid to ask.

I did not know how much I wanted his answer to be yes and now if it isn't yes I think my heart is going to shatter into a thousand pieces.

Why the hell did I ask that? he doesn't love me. We only just met a short while ago. This is just a fling. Nothing more. An adventure. A mistake.

What was I thinking?

Panic surges inside me.

It's hard to keep my face calm enough to hide the turmoil erupting in my body.

He chuckles, brushing hair away from eyes. His fingers trailing over my skin and sparking desire inside me.

"I would tear this fucking world to pieces for you. Yes. I am in love with you." His answer is a dark whisper of truth. An underground river, moving in below the surface of my body.

Even if I wanted to, I wouldn't have been able to hide my happiness and relief at hearing his response. My body melts against him and I grab his face in my hands and kiss him hard.

Charged energy sparks between us, fueling my body, screaming through my soul.

I'm in love with Rufino Vece.

From the moment I laid eyes on him, it was him. We are destined to be together. Fate threw us into that moment and now no one can tear us apart.

I love him.

And now I know he loves me too.

Love.

"Dance with me." He says, pushing me towards the velvet curtain and down stairs to the dance floor.

Somewhere in the back of my mind I remember my bodyguards are here with their eyes on me, annoyed that I disappeared for a while - but maybe they won't recognize Rufino for who he is. Just another guy in the club on the dance floor with me. It's hard to care about idiots watching you when your heart is overflowing with excitement and wonder.

I've never been in love before.

I've always run from it. Hesitated when it presented itself or just flat out denied its existence. No one was ever up to the task of impressing me.

Rufino doesn't give me the choice. I can't stop myself from being in love with him. There is no control. Only wild, exhilarating, dangerous *love*.

I move against him, dancing and touching, grinning to myself as the bright colorful lights flash over our skin and in the thin layer of smoke settled over the dance floor.

This might just be the biggest adventure I've ever been on.

"I don't want to go yet." I whine a little, leaning against his chest near the exit doors of the club. Tucked just out of view from where I spotted the two personal guards standing outside.

"It's late, little vixen. We can see each other tomorrow." He says, kissing my forehead. It is late. And I'm exhausted. It's been a long, magical night. I want to go home with him though. It doesn't seem fair that I should have to walk away from the man I am in love with.

He tilts my chin up with his long fingers and gently kisses my lips.

"Text me when you get home."

I wrap my arms around his neck and pull him closer, kissing him again.

"Promise you'll see me tomorrow." I whisper.

"I promise."

He doesn't walk me out because it would be too risky. But I can feel him watching me from the doorway as I walk towards the waiting Uber.

In the car I can't stop smiling. This doesn't seem real.

I'm filled with a mix of excitement and tension. We took so many risks tonight and I'm not sure what my security guards did or didn't see. I can only hope that they didn't recognize Red and don't go reporting my activities to my father.

The worst thing that could happen right now would be for my father to find out. He's threatened so many times to send me away. I would die if he sent me away now - when I found love. When I finally found Red.

"Here you go, miss." The driver says and I realize I have been lost in my thoughts for the past few minutes. I didn't even know I had arrived at home.

"Thank you." I say, climbing out of the Uber, glancing over my shoulder as I walk into the building.

The security guards are parking their car to follow me inside.

I roll my eyes, punching the elevator button harder and harder to try make it arrive faster before they can get here so I don't have to ride up with them.

Unfortunately, one of them climbed out before the other parked and he shoves his hand in the closing door just in time to stop it. He steps inside with me and I huff.

He doesn't say a word as the doors slide closed and we move upwards.

His eyes are locked onto me though - as though he knows something I don't.

His phone rings, and he pulls it out to answer it.

"Yes, sir. We have arrived home. Yes, sir."

He slides it back into his pocket.

"Was that my father?"

He doesn't answer. Asshole.

The elevator doors slide open and he pushes me gently out of the lift and into the penthouse.

My father is awake and standing in the living room with his arms folded across his chest. His eyes are dark, tainted with anger and disapproval.

"Are you drunk?" he snarls.

I sigh heavily.

"I'm tired, and I'm going to bed."

"Where were you, Verity?"

"Clubbing with the girls." I sigh.

"Why don't you answer me truthfully for once? Just try it out, see how it feels." He is pushing my patience.

"I *really was clubbing*." I moan. "Ask one of these idiots." I gesture over the security guys.

My father steps forward and hands me his iPad.

"Huh?" I mutter, taking it from him, not sure what he wants me to do with it.

He raises his brows and gestures towards the screen.

Sighing, I look down at the device in my hand and my heart sinks to the pit of my stomach. For a moment I can't breathe.

It's a media site. A popular one.

And the primary image on the front page is a photograph of Rufino and me - kissing outside a restaurant. A stolen kiss, I remember it. Quick, risky - we laughed afterwards.

Now it has become a crisp image for the entire world to gawk at.

Fuck.

I take a while to pluck up the courage to lift my eyes off the screen and up towards my father.

The veins on his temple are popping out in thick ridges like blue snakes lying beneath his skin. Pulsing as the blood throbs through them.

His eyes are dark orbs of disgust - aimed at me.

I don't think I've ever seen him *this* angry before.

I tear my eyes away from him and set the iPad down on the coffee table.

It's too heavy - the evidence of what I've been doing is a weight I don't want to hold in front of my father.

"What the fuck is wrong with you, Verity?" He snarls.

"I love him." I blurt out. Immediately knowing it was the worst thing I could ever have said.

"You - you - *love him*?" He screams, his neck muscle taunt and his fists clenched. "You are trying to tell me you *love* that savage degenerate. Our enemy. Are you fucking *stupid*?"

My insides are churning, my mind torn. Fight back, defend the man I love, or keep my mouth shut to try to make this situation at least a fraction easier.

But anger is surging inside me now.

Anger about every time my father has tried to control me - every time he's manipulated my life and taken things away from me. Every time he's tried to tell me who I had to be and stopped me from being myself.

That anger bubbles up from inside me and floods out of my mouth in a tidal wave.

"I don't care what you think. I don't care if you aren't happy to call me your daughter. Red accepts me for who I am. He loves me for *who I am*. Not who he wishes I was. I don't care if you're angry. I don't care about anything."

I scream and I can feel the tension in the room growing. Security guards take a polite step backwards, creating space between themselves and my rage.

"You don't care." My father's voice is so low I feel my skin crawl with fear.

I bite my lip, glaring at him, too scared to speak again, but too frustrated to back down.

"We will see if you care when I send you to Europe to live in the convent."

I gasp.

"Break it off with him, Verity. End it. Or that is where you are going. I am sick and tired of your fucking games. You've pushed it too far this time. I'm not stupid. This isn't love. This is you trying to piss me off. I see it for what it is. Now end it. Or I'm booking your flight."

He spins away from me, his fists still clenched as he marches towards his room. I can't move.

My heart is racing.

My skin is on fire.

Salty tears blurred my eyes.

One of the security guards clears his throat and I turn my anger onto him.

"Was that fun? Did you enjoy the fucking show?"

He presses his lips together, his arms folded over his chest.

I storm away from them and their pitiful stares. I don't want people pitying me. Especially not *those* assholes.

CHAPTER EIGHT
Rufino

My phone is blowing up on the drive home.

The constant influx of message chimes makes me grin, thinking it must be Verity contacting me, but when I glance at the notifications, I see a string of messages from my brothers.

Fuck.

No.

What the fuck? I am not in the mood for any more of their shit.

Its Saturday night. Or, Sunday morning. There is no fucking way they should be messaging me about work shit now. They're probably still pissed off about me leaving the meeting. But still - it's an odd time to be messaging me.

Ignoring the messages until I pull up in my underground parking area I sigh, flicking open the app.

Oh.

Masaccio has tried to call me several times during the night, but I didn't hear while I was in the club. So he resorted to messaging me - an image that sends a thrill through my body. Both tension and excitement.

The truth is out.

There is a screenshot of a news article staring back at me.

A photograph.

Verity has her hand on my chest, her face tilted upwards, her long wavy hair flowing down her back - and her lips pressed against mine.

It's a stunning photo. We are incredible together.

But my brothers aren't in the same mind frame.

While I'm looking at the screenshot my phone rings.

A low groan of annoyances rumbles through me. The last thing I want to do now is talk to Masaccio.

I flick the call away, declining it, knowing it will only cause more shit later on, but I want to at least get upstairs first.

He calls back immediately.

Each time the ringer goes off I can feel his tension from the other side of the call. It is just getting worse the longer I delay this.

With a heavy sigh I answer.

"Rufino?" He snaps.

"Here."

"What the fuck is going on are you fucking kidding me with this fucking bullshit are you trying to start a fucking war or something? I can hardly make out the words amidst the anger they are spewing. He is screaming into the phone and I have to hold it away from my face.

It's better not to speak now. Let him vent. Let him get it all out of his system. Just listen.

His opinion doesn't mean shit to me.

He can dictate the best options for the business - but he needs to stay the fuck out of my personal life.

I sigh and he carries on telling me I'm a complete fuck up and have no regard for the safety of our family.

By the time I get upstairs into my penthouse apartment I'm almost ready to hang up. He's vented enough.

I've allowed him this outlet and now I'm over it.

"Masaccio."

I try to interrupt him, but he ignores it.

"And what about how this will affect —"

"Masaccio, can you stop for a second?" I snarl, getting more annoyed.

"You are so inconsiderate."

I can't take another second of this.

Hanging up the phone I toss it onto the sofa. Then on second thoughts, I pick it up again and put it on silent. He's already trying to call me back.

I'm too tired for this. A shower and some sleep is all I really need right now.

I had the most incredible night with Verity and for it to end this way is like a knife in my back.

Although - is this really as bad as it seems to be?

Maybe now that it's out in the open we don't have to sneak around anymore.

I should call Verity and warn her, but she might be sleeping. I'll let her rest and we can talk about it in the morning, rather.

I can't stop her father from finding out, so there's no use panicking.

Whatever happens from here on out - I will deal with it.

The only thing that matters is that Verity and I both feel the same way about each other.

Whether it's love or obsession - or just the thrill of wanting to be with the one girl I can't have - I don't care.

I want her.

She belongs to me.

Sleep comes quickly because it's been a long day and an amazing night. But my dreams are a messy, confusing, broken story of chaos.

In one I am chasing a car, running down the road screaming her name as she turns to look at me through the back window, tears streaming down her cheeks.

In another we are on an island, but the island is filled with snakes and we have to leave.

Some of my family are there, but they all hate me. In others it's her father, setting fires and trying to keep her from me.

When I wake up in the morning, I'm not rested. I am heavy with emotion and confusion.

The only thing I'm sure of is that I want to see her.

Rolling over in bed I grumble, wishing I could close my eyes and go back to sleep for a few more hours, but once I'm awake, I can never go back to sleep. So, I throw off the blankets and head down stairs to make some coffee. I'm almost at the kitchen when I hear the front door slamming open.

"What the fuck?" I mutter to myself, walking through to see what the hell is going on.

Masaccio and Tuomo are standing just inside the doorway. Celso is standing behind them.

"Oh for fuck sakes." I grumble, making my opinion on their presence here very clear.

"Why aren't you answering your phone?" Tuomo demands.

I gesture towards where the phone is lying on the sofa. "It's on silent, because I knew you assholes wouldn't let me sleep tonight."

"Do you understand you are making dangerous choices just chasing down some temporary thrill? You are risking everything for a little excitement."

"It's not temporary."

"Are you fucking serious? This has to end. Right now."

"Not happening." I wave my hand in dismissal.

Masaccio takes a very aggressive step towards me and Tuomo steps in front of him blocking him off. "That will not help. We have to deal with the situation at hand - he safety of the family."

"I want to kill him." Mas snarls.

"Get in line." I taunt him, walking back towards the kitchen because if I have to deal with this I need coffee. A double shot of expresso.

I should never have given them spare keys to my place. That was for emergencies. Not breaking and entering.

I want the coffee to taste amazing, but I'm too annoyed to enjoy it.

Sitting in the living room I'm listening to my brothers switch between telling me what a selfish asshole I am - and trying to make a pre-emptive plan against whatever Verity's father is going to do when he finds out if he hasn't already - which I'm sure he has.

I feel like I'm sitting in the middle of some twisted intervention.

They are each judging my life and my choices as

though none of them have ever done a single wrong thing in the course of their existence.

While they talk back and forth between themselves I message Verity. Hoping they'll just leave.

> Me: Hi gorgeous, we're famous. Is your dad furious? Are you ok?

> Verity: He's furious. He told me if I didn't end it with you he was going to send me to Europe.

> Me: I won't let that happen. I want to see you. Can you get out this afternoon?

> Verity: Sure, but it's going to be harder to lose the guards.

We decide that the best place to meet is the broad walk along the waterfront. It's a busy place and we can blend in to the crowds or slip away if we can manage it.

After talking to Verity for a while I open some news sites, just to get an idea of what we are dealing with. Our photo is everywhere. Not just the first one I saw, but others too. Us in a club, walking down the street, at the yacht club. There is zero chance of being able to call it a once off mistake.

Not that I wanted to.

I'm still enjoying the fact that the truth is out.

I haven't figure out how yet, but I am going to be with her.

♥

Warm wind stirs against my shirt. Glancing over at the water I clench my jaw, trying to figure out the best way that her and I can be together.

I sense her and turn in her direction.

Verity walks nervously towards me, glancing over her shoulder to check if anyone is following, then looking back my way and grinning.

"I can't believe I lost them." She laughs, jumping into my arms.

"Are you alright?" I ask, hugging her against me and burying my nose against her hair to soak smell her.

"Ugh, yes, my dad lectured me last night and then it started all over again his morning. He went on for hours. I thought my ears were going to fall off. Honestly, it's a little over the top to threaten to send me away. I don't think he will. He would miss me too much." She giggles.

"Don't worry - I got the same bullshit lectures from my brothers. Fuck them. It's you and me against the world. I meant what I said last night, Verity."

Her big green eyes pierce into me. Her lashes lowered and her gaze intense.

"That I love you." I smirk.

"You do? Are you serious?" She says, feigning surprise.

"Watch yourself." I laugh, holding her even tighter. She giggles and snuggles against me, her body curved into mine.

When she looks at me this time, her eyes are softer. "I love you too, Red. I don't care what my father says. I won't give this up."

"We just need to be a little more careful until we can figure out a way around this." As I say it I see the reporter taking a photograph of us. His long camera lens looks heavy.

"Hey." I shout, making a move towards him, but the guy takes off running full speed away from us.

"Was that a reporter?" She asks, not sounding as concerned as I thought she would.

"Yes. So much for being more careful. I don't think it matters where we go at this point. It's not your security guards we have to avoid, it's *everyone*."

"Ugh. I can already sense another lecture coming from my father." She rolls her eyes. "Well, we may as well just enjoy the afternoon then. Do you want to get something to eat?"

I can't help the smile that steals its way onto my face. She really doesn't give a fuck about anything. Her attitude is fucking sexy.

"Come on, little vixen, I could do with a beer and a steak right now." Taking her hand we walk together towards one of the popular restaurants this side of town. Neither of us is looking around at who might be watching. We're too lost in each other.

For a moment I wonder if Masaccio was right.

Am I just in this for the thrill of it? I am addicted to the danger of being with Verity?

No.

It's more than that. Our connection is something unique that I've never felt before. I've never met anyone like her.

There is no chance in hell I am letting her go.

CHAPTER NINE
Verity

The security guards are waiting for me at the penthouse when I arrive home later that afternoon. I had a wonderful day with Red. I knew that by the time I got back here there would be extra press out about us so when my father is waiting at the front door to confront me with the same question he asked yesterday - this time I am honest about it.

"Where the fuck were you?" He snarls.

"With Rufino at the waterfront." I say, tossing my purse onto the sofa and flopping down onto the soft pillows to prepare for the inevitable lecture that is about to ensue. I may as well get comfortable whilst waiting for it.

My father stands over me, looking down with that all too familiar expression of disapproval and disappointment on his face.

I hate that look.

I see it all the time.

It's like when he looks at me he never seems me for who I am. He never sees *me*. Only what he wishes I was and all the things I'm not.

He *makes* me want to rebel just by giving me that look.

"I've given you more than enough chances to show me you can be a lady - or anything other than a defiant, reckless, selfish spoilt brat, Verity."

"Jeez, calm down. I honestly think you're overreacting a bit here."

"Overreacting?" he screams. "Your face is all over the media *again*. Right after I told you to break it off."

"Daddy."

"Don't fucking *daddy* me. I don't want to listen to it. This is over. You are not leaving the house." He gestures towards the two security guards standing nearby. "You two - she is now on lockdown inside this house. She is not to leave under any circumstances. Do I make myself clear?"

"Yes, sir." They reply in unison, nodding like obedient soldiers.

"Dad."

He spins and points his finger at me, the snarl on his lip curving it up so high I can see his teeth. He's beyond furious. This is not good. The red veins along his temple are popping blue now and it looks like he's about to have a heart attack his eyes are so wild.

I press my lips together and swallow hard.

Say nothing, Verity. You are asking for more trouble. try to talk to him tomorrow, rather. Give him a chance to calm down and then you can smooth this over.

I sit still on the sofa, unsure about what I should do.

My father is still glaring at me.

I nod three short quick nods. A submissive gesture in his eyes.

With one last glare thrown in my direction he storms out of the living room.

I breathe a massive sigh of relief and grab my phone, running to my room and slamming the door.

He doesn't really mean it. He wouldn't lock me in this house.

I'll wait a day or two and suss out his mood then I'll be able to smooth this away like I always do.

I flop face first down onto my bed and groan into my pillow.

This whole thing is a mess.

People should just learn to mind their own business. I'm an adult but my father still treats me like a child, as though I'm not free to make any choices for myself.

If I stretch my arm towards the bedside table, I can just reach my phone without having to get up.

The bright light makes me squint so I turn it down a little and then open the messaging app to talk to Rufino.

For so long now I have been alone.

Yes, I have great friends who I love to party with - but I don't have someone who understands me. Someone who sees me. Not just the party version of me. But *me*.

I don't know what it is about Red that makes me so comfortable around him. I love how he not only puts up with my snarky comments but grins at them and then gives back as hard as I throw out.

He really challenges me and push me in ways I've never felt before.

Right now, all I want to do is to be around him.

I think it's cruel that my father wants to keep us apart. Why wouldn't he want me to feel this love?

> Me: Hi sexy, I miss you already.

>> Rufino: Hey gorgeous girl. I miss you too. Did all hell break loose when you got home? I saw the new articles.

> Me: Yes, my father is turning into a lunatic. He said I'm not allowed to leave the house. But I think he'll calm down by tomorrow. He always overreacts about things.

> Rufino: Mm. I don't like the sound of that. He can't keep you from me.

> Me: Don't worry about it. I'll talk to him tomorrow. But for now…I took a little picture for you.

I giggle, sitting up on the bed and pulling my top off, then snapping a cheeky photo for him. I hit send and grin while I wait for his response.

> Rufino: If you keep sending photos like that I am going to have to break into your bedroom tonight while you're sleeping and tie you up so I can do whatever I want to you.

My heart races and my mind runs wild.

> Me: Well, maybe I'll leave the window unlocked. But it's on the top floor so kind of impossible for you to get to.

> Rufino: I think you underestimate just how much I want your body against mine. There is no such thing as impossible.

Talking to Rufino makes me forget the fight I had with my father.

Our messages go back and forth for hours before I'm too tired to keep my eyes open.

After saying goodnight I curl up hugging my pillow against my body and wishing it was him lying next to me.

When I close my eyes I fantasize about him doing crazy things to reach me because he's so in love with me. I've never had someone treat me this way. Someone who makes me feel like they really would tear the world apart to be with me.

There is a tapping sound drifting into my dream and pulling me awake. I blink in the darkness of my bedroom and realize that the white curtains are catching a breeze from my open window. I could have sworn I closed it.

I sigh, sleepy and comfortable, pulling the blankets a little tighter over my shoulders.

But then I feel it.

And my heart races with fear.

Someone is in my room.

My eyes shoot open and I see the tall, dark figure standing next to my bed.

"Don't be afraid, vixen." A deep voice whispers, ominous.

I open my mouth to scream for help but a massive hand clamps over my face.

"If your guards come running in here, I will be forced to kill them - I don't want to do that," he growls in warning.

I stare at him with wide eyes, full of fear and - desire.

He grabs the edge of my blanket and pulls it off my body. Exposing my naked skin to the crisp, cool air.

A low rumbling sound vibrates through his chest and sends shivers down my spine.

I mumble against his hand, my words are muffled and inaudible.

"Sshhhh." His breath is hot against my ear as he leans over me. "I'm not here to talk." His hand brushes up my leg, over the inside of my thigh.

I squirm and kick him away and his eyes flash with excitement.

"I was hoping you would put up a fight." He laughs.

Using his free hand he yanks his belt loose and my body tingles with anticipation, eyeing the bulge pushing up against the crotch of his pants.

"Don't make a sound." He snarls, lifting his hand off my mouth.

Rufino wraps the belt around my wrists and through the bedpost above my head.

I whimper when he yanks his pants open, standing over me so that I can see the full size of his cock.

His shirt is hanging open, those gorgeous sculpted muscles running over his stomach and dipping down towards his cock are making me crazy with lust.

He grabs my legs roughly and pulls them open, kneeling between my thighs.

I squirm away and he grins.

His hands dig into my hips as he pins me down, lying his body over mine.

I take a sharp breath in, but before I can let out a sound, he clamps his hand around my throat and presses hard enough to cut off my voice.

Then his cock slams into me.

My pupils dilate with pleasure when he pulls out and slams into me again.

Lightheaded dizziness swims through my head, my air restricted just enough to make me feint. Under his control, I am completely defenseless.

He is still fucking me, his cock forcing my pussy wide open every time he pushes deep inside me.

Grunts of pleasure sound against my ear from his forceful thrusts.

"Fuck, you are so perfect, I will never let you go." He moans while he fucks me.

My legs shake.

I arch my hips upwards.

His cock slides in and out of my pussy and the sensations all become overwhelming.

An orgasm crashes into me like a tidal wave.

Washing through my entire body, ripping me open and leaving my lying bare.

He goes rock hard inside me and I feel the pulsing release of his own pleasure.

I wake up with a smile on my face, wanting to go back to sleep and return to the dream.

My body is tingling with the remnants of how he made me feel. The excitement. The delightful games I want to play with him.

Glancing at my phone I see it's already past nine.

My legs flex as I stretch them out beneath the blankets. It's time for coffee. A shower. A new day.

Padding my way down to the kitchen, still trying to yawn away the last drowsy faded bits of sleep, I have a silly smile on my face.

My father looks up at me from the coffee station.

"Morning, daddy." I mumble sweetly.

He grunts his response, picking up his coffee and turning towards me.

"Your flight is booked and paid for. You leave on Thursday night."

My heart stops cold in my chest.

"Leave?" I rub my eyes, trying to force myself

awake and deal with the thick vein of fear that has flooded my veins.

"I warned you, Verity. And now you will have to deal with the consequences." He says coldly.

"Leave to where?" I say, my voice reaching a higher octave as panic tightens my throat.

"To the convent."

"Daddy, I'm sorry, can we talk about this? You don't have to send me away, it was just a silly."

"It's done, Verity. The time for talking is over. You had your chance. You made your choice."

He walks out of the kitchen, and I grab his arm. "Daddy."

"Get your fucking hands off me." He snarls in anger and I wince away from him.

I've never seen that look on his face before.

Frozen in place my bare feet are cold against the marble floor. But not as cold as the thread of fear and anger mixing inside me. I don't know what to do. There is no fucking way I am going to go live in a convent. Not a chance. I have to find a way out of this.

I have to convince my father to change his mind.

Taking the stairs two at a time I run back up to my room and grab my phone.

> Me: My father has booked my flight to Europe. He is sending me to live in a convent. I'm leaving on Thursday.

My stomach is churning with worry.

> Rufino: I will never let that happen, vixen. You are not going anywhere. I will fix this.

> Me: What are you going to do?

> Rufino: Let me worry about that.

A thrill of fear and excitement pulses through me.

But I also know my father. He will never change his mind. There is no chance in hell that Rufino is going to talk him out of this.

As much as I want to believe there is a way out - I also accept my fate. My father is a powerful man.

He always gets what he wants.

I have just under a week before my entire life is going to change for the worst.

Over dinner that evening, under the watchful gaze of my reinforced set of body guards, I try to convince my father to let me enjoy one last weekend of fun before my life comes to a devastating end.

"I want to go to Vegas this weekend - with Sammy and Bella."

"I said no." He snaps.

"Daddy, I'll have four security guards with me. You won't have to worry about anything. Please, I won't even complain when you put me on the plane to Europe if you let me have this last weekend in Vegas." I pout my lip a little, trying to plead with my eyes.

My father sighs heavily and drops his fork on his plate.

"Fuck sakes. Fine. One weekend. But those security guards are going *everywhere* with you."

I jump out, eager and looking forward to the weekend.

But as Vegas gets closer, the anger does too. This will be my *last weekend of freedom.* I can't believe he is doing this to me.

CHAPTER TEN
Rufino

Celso is hopping back and forth from foot to foot, already hyped up and eager to climb into the ring.

It was the perfect stroke of luck when my brothers invited me for a weekend in Vegas to watch Celso fight in the big MMA event that's happening here.

The perfect cover reason for being here.

Of course, I've hardly been paying any attention to the fights at all.

My eyes have been on her all evening.

She is sitting on the other side of the ring surrounded by friends and too many guards. And she's drunk.

Verity has been screaming at the fighters, pushing spectators around her and being belligerent. She's angry. I don't blame her. I would be furious too if my father was planning to ship me away to Europe to live with a bunch of nuns under tight controlling rules.

I chuckle when she tosses her drink in some guys face and slaps him.

Fucking feisty when she's angry.

And even more sexy.

Every now and then our eyes meet and my heart beats faster. A sly grin crossing my lips.

She bites her lower lip and smiles at me.

This is the only type of interaction we've had since I arrived. It's driving me crazy to not be able to walk over there and grab her in my arms.

But for now - this is what I need to do. I need to keep my distance and bide my time until the right opportunity presents itself.

I'm not in Vegas for the fight, or the drinks or the party.

I'm here for one reason and one reason only.

Her.

There is no fucking way I am letting her father send her to Europe and I have just the plan to stop it from happening.

"Hey, he's going in." Tuomo slaps me excitedly on my back and points his chin towards Celso who he walking towards the fight ring.

"Hells ye." I cheer him on, blending in and giving them no reason to think I am up to anything at all. "What's his opponent like?"

"Fast. And dangerous. But Celso is faster. It's going to be a close fight though." Masaccio says, tilting his beer back and downing half of it.

Tuomo chuckles. "He's going to be hurting after this."

"Nothing a few drinks won't solve at the afterparty." Mas laughs.

I glance from Mas to Tuomo and then across the ring to Celso. For the briefest of moments I feel like I am part of the family. A sense of belonging I've been craving all my life. But it's fleeting. Disintegrating before it takes hold inside of me.

It's easy to pretend though. Just for now.

Until I can make my move.

The ref stands between Celso and his opponent.

"Let's have a clean fight." He shouts, then steps back and blows his whistle to show the start of this round.

Neither Celso nor his opponent waste even a second of time. They both fly forward, attacking with force and energy.

Celso drops low at the last second and swings his fist up towards the other guys chin, connecting with a snap and causing his head to jolt backwards.

The crowd erupts in screaming chaos.

A thick layer of goosebumps spreads across my arms.

It's exhilarating.

It's so raw to watch them beat the living shit out of each other and have thousands of people scream encouragement at them.

I didn't anticipate getting so involved in the fight, but as each moment passes, I become excited about it.

Celso is fucking good.

Tuomo was right. His opponent is fast, but Celso is faster.

A spinning kick to the head sends Celso flying across the mat.

I hold my breath, waiting for him to get up.

Tuomo and Mas are shouting next to me. "Get up. Get the fuck up."

Just as his opponent reaches him Celso kicks upwards and sends the guy stumbling away. Then he's back on his feet and I feel a current of relief.

When Celso takes the guy down, it's brutal.

He hits him so hard his mouth guard goes flying out of his mouth, somewhere into the crowd. The guy spins and lands flat on his face, not moving.

The ref counts and the entire crowd is silent, holding their breath, waiting.

"Winner." The ref shouts, grabbing Celso's hand and lifting it high into the air. My brothers are going crazy next to me, jumping and cheering.

I stare across the ring towards Verity. She licks her lips and runs her fingertips over her collar bone. My cock stirs and heat burns beneath my skin.

Soon, vixen.

One of her friends grabs her arm and pulls her from her seat. I hear her shouting something about the afterparty.

Verity glances towards me. I nod. She grins, then lets her friend pull her away. Four security guards moving along behind her. Her father really went out of his way to make sure she wasn't doing anything he didn't approve of this weekend.

But her father doesn't understand how determined I am.

The afterparty is pulsing with energy.

People are packed against each other that it's almost impossible to push our way towards the bar.

"Tequila." Celso says grinning. His left eye is already turning blue underneath it and his lip is split.

"Better get you two - by the looks of you." I laugh.

Mas and Tuomo are standing behind us, looking annoyed. They aren't used to the clubbing scene. "Let's get a VIP table." Mas leans forward and shouts.

"Go for it. Message me when you've organized something, and I'll come join you."

He nods and pushes away from us, Tuomo following him.

Celso and I stay at the bar and I watch him throw back four tequilas. His adrenalin is still so high from the fight - those drinks are going to knock him flat on his face or send him in a wild party mood.

"Three vodka shots."

I hear her voice to my left and my body responds.

Turning towards her my eyes trace over her gorgeous features. Her hair is pinned up in a messy bun, glitter powders her long dark lashes, and a very dark red paint colors her full lips.

She looks fucking gorgeous.

Verity eyes me across the bar, throwing me looks only I understand.

But it's clear what she wants from me.

Someone behind her bumps her and she turns to face them and with a snarl and swing of her elbow she clocks the guy right in his jaw.

"What the fuck?" Someone screams. Chaos breaks out and two body guards pile towards her to pull her away from it.

She's fucking pissed off.

And she's taking it out on everyone around her.

My eyes follow her as they pull her away from the bar back to the table she has near the dance floor.

Celso mumbles something to me.

"What?"

"They've got a table." He says again. His eyes are already glaring over from the shots.

"Go ahead. I'll see you there now. I'm just going to have another drink here first."

"Suite yourself. It's there to the left of the dance floor."

He points and I nod. Celso pushes his way away from the bar and through the crowds towards where my other brothers are sitting.

The tables have been cornered off to reduce chaos around them, but the place is so full that even the VIP area demands maneuvering to get anywhere.

My eyes drift off my brothers and back to where Verity is sitting. Except she's not sitting. She's standing on the table with a bottle of vodka in her hand, dancing and laughing.

Her hips swaying and her dress flexing over her gorgeous curves.

One of her friends tries to pull her off the table and she swats them away.

A security guard steps forward and with his hands on her waist he lifts her off the table.

I want to punch him in the face for touching her.

No one touches her but me.

But I stand my ground. Now is not the time.

Verity is fighting with the security guard now, trying to punch him as well, but he's much bigger than her and it looks like a kitten trying to fight a lion.

He sits her down on the sofa and steps away.

She huffs and tilts the bottle of vodka to her lips, drinking way more than she should.

As the evening goes on I watch her, waiting, calm, excited and nervous. The mix of emotions running through me are all overrun by my patience - which is wearing thin.

My brothers have given up trying to get me to sit with them and have left me at the bar. They still don't know Verity is here, and that's fine with me.

Then I see it.

My chance.

Verity gets up and makes her way towards the VIP bathrooms.

I push through the crowd ahead of her. I have to get into the bathroom before her security guards get there.

It's the only place they don't go, but they will wait right by the door once she is inside.

I move aggressively through the crowd, pushing people out of the way and sending them stumbling and shouting in annoyance.

I run down the passage towards the end where it splits left towards the females side.

Bolting around a corner I pin my back up against a wall, waiting.

Verity is arguing with the guard escorting her as she stumbles towards the corner.

"Ugh. Just wait here." She huffs.

"I need to check inside the bathroom." He says.

"Are you crazy? There are girls in there. Don't be a savage." She says in horror.

There is a moment of tense silence and then he sighs. "I am waiting right over here. Try nothing."

"It's the only way out, idiot. I will not stay in the bathroom all night just to escape you."

He lets out an agitated growl and I chuckle, trying to imagine how little patience he has left after having to deal with a drunk, out-of-control Verity all night.

She walks straight past me without seeing me.

Stumbling into one stall she closes the door and I hear her sighing.

When I'm one hundred percent sure the security guard will not change his mind and follow her in I move away from my hiding place and grab the door of her stall and yank it open. The little slip lock snaps free of the wall far too easily and I am suddenly staring down at Verity, sitting on the toilet with a shocked expression on her face.

Then she giggles.

"I'm trying to pee here." She sniggers.

I grin.

"Well, hurry up. We don't have a lot of time."

CHAPTER ELEVEN
Verity

I flop down onto the toilet seat muttering about the stupid security and the stupid trip to Europe and the stupid people at the after party.

My head is spinning, tainted by far too many vodkas and I can barely see straight.

But I feel pretty fucking good.

"Las Vegas, baby." I giggle to myself.

Suddenly the door of my toilet stall bursts open and I'm about to let out an ear-piercing scream when I look up and see Rufino. At first I don't understand. My little brain is spasming trying to work out what is going on.

But he smiles at me and my heart flip flops and a massive grin spreads across my face too.

"I'm trying to pee here." I giggle.

"Well, hurry. We don't have a lot of time."

I wiggle my dress back down over my hips and almost fall over in the tight space of the stall.

Rufino grabs my waist and steadies me.

"Hey sexy." I giggle again. "What are you doing here?"

"I'm kidnapping you." He says, sounding serious as fuck. I laugh again, but when I look into his eyes, I can see he isn't joking.

"You can't kidnap me. I have too many security people." I wave my hand towards the other side of the door - where the guard is waiting. A little hiccup makes me blink in surprise.

"They won't even notice you're gone until it's too late." He says, sounding like he knows what he's talking about.

He pulls me out of the stall and into the main room.

Rufino is leading me towards the other side of the ladies powder area and then before I know it he's lifted me up to a massive window.

"Hey." I complain, wiggling in his grip.

"Climb through." He says and I gasp in shock.

"You want me to climb through the window?" I say, sounding defiant.

"Yes, Verity. Slide your legs through and lower yourself down on the other side. It's not high at all.

He holds me while I maneuver my legs through and then roll onto my stomach to slide down to the ground on the other side. I look at the window, grinning proudly at my sneaky ninja ability. I'm no longer in the ladies bathroom.

I giggle again and grip the wall tightly while the world carries on spinning.

Everything seems funny right now.

Rufino climbs through the window after me, but *he* makes it seem easy.

I squint at him trying to determine his true intentions with all of this.

He must be playing some kind of game.

It's clear he won't *kidnap* me.

That would be insane.

No one is that crazy.

"Are you ok?" he asks, looking down at me. I nod.

Rufino takes my hand and starts walking too fast down a hallway. I stumble in my stilettos and grumble that he needs to slow down. He growls and bends down to scoop me up, cradling me in his arms.

"Where are we going for real though?" I ask with slurred words, wondering why he seems so tense.

"You'll see." He replies, focused on other things.

I can barely focus on his face never mind where he is carrying me off to.

Before I know it we are outside in the fresh night air. Bright, colorful lights shine from the surrounding buildings. Casinos, night clubs, restaurants - all trying to entice us to come inside.

A gorgeous girl walks past wearing nothing but feathers.

I grin and wave at her.

But Rufino doesn't seem to be interested in any of it - instead he yanks open the door of a car and sets me down in the passenger seat.

I knot my brows, worrying that maybe this isn't a game. My father is going to freak out when he finds out I've ditched the guards.

He'll upgrade my convent stay from a nice comfortable room to a prison cell in their basement.

I wiggle in my seat, freaking out for a second. I grip the door handle with my fingers. Push it open. Get out. Go back inside. That's the right choice to make.

But I am awful at making right choices.

My father constantly reminds me how terrible I am as a daughter.

I *should* go back inside - but the idea of my father finding out I ditched the guards sends a wild thrill through me. I giggle and when Rufino climbs into the driver's side he glances over at me. "Are you laughing?" he asks. I let go of the door handle and settle into the seat.

"This is fun." I grin.

He raises one eyebrow at me. "I'm glad you see it that way."

The engine roars to life, and he wheel spins away from the casino that was hosting the afterparty.

I glance behind us, trying to see out the back window, but all I can make out is a colorful mess of neon lights blurring into each other.

"No one is following us." He says confidently, skidding around a corner.

"Then why are you in such a rush?"

"Because the sooner we get this part of it done the happier I will be."

"What part of what?"

He smirks and I can see he will not tell me. He's enjoying this too much now. Escaping the guards was the hard part - the rest of it is the fun part by the looks of things.

I press the window button, winding it all the way down, leaning my head out of the window and letting the window whip my hair loose around my face I scream, "This is Las Vegas, baby."

This is the most exciting thing I've ever done.

I am fully aware of how stupid it is.

I'm drunk, not an idiot - but I don't care.

It's my last weekend of freedom and now I get to spend it with Rufino.

The car comes to a stop outside a tall building with a giant neon heart glowing half way up the side of it.

"Come on." He says, pulling my door open and taking my hand.

He leads me inside and my stomach knots.

"Is this?" I turn in a circle, trying to take it all in but the colors are swimming and moving about too much.

"It's a wedding chapel, vixen. We're getting married."

"Married?" I shout too loud, shock pulsing through me like electricity. I can't get married. I'm only twenty-three. No ways. This is a *stupid* idea.

I turn to face Rufino my eyes wide with panic spilling from them.

He grins, grabs my jaw in his hand and kisses me.

The moment our lips touch my mind goes silent.

It's a beautiful sensation of complete calm, then a crazy rush of passion. I wrap my arms around his neck and pull myself closer against him. My body belongs to him. Of course, I will marry him. We're in Vegas, baby.

He kisses me until I am melted against him, until I've lost all sense of control. The control I never had to begin with.

"Let's get ready." He says, stepping away, but keeping his arm locked around my waist.

In a room to the side of the chapel he searches through racks of white dresses.

Pulling one out at a time and holding it up against me. Finally, he hands me a short, tight lacey body hugging dress.

"In there - put it on." He points to a change room.

"Okie dokie." I grin and stumble over my foot, grateful when he catches me.

In the change room I wiggle out of my blue and pink dress, holding onto the wall, and into the white lace wedding dress. This *is* fun. And crazy and wild and adventurous.

I can't believe he wants to marry me.

For real.

Vegas weddings *are* real. Many people don't understand that.

I slip my high heels back onto my feet and do my best to leave the change room looking elegant and not falling on my face again.

Rufino's smile takes my breath away when he sees me.

His eyes graze over me and he shakes his head. "Fuck me, you look incredible." He says, pulling me up against his broad, muscular chest.

"Your hair is a bit wild though." He laughs, turning me around.

Half of the bun came out when I put my head out of the car window.

Rufino pulls my hair tie loose and brushes his fingers though my messy curls. He pulls it all up on top of my head and back into the not-as-messy-as-before bun.

When I turn around to face him again, he is holding out a little crystal box, cut from a pink stone, sitting on the palm of his hand and glittering in the light.

"What is this?" I ask, taking it from his hand.

"Your engagement ring."

I flick the box open. Inside the carved out belly of the stone is a ring. It's also pink, glittering the same way the box is glittering.

"It's rose quartz, set in sterling silver. It's all they had here at the chapel. I will get you a proper ring later on. We can choose it together. But we need one for tonight."

"Are you kidding me? I *love* this one. I don't need another one. This one is perfect." I grin, slipping it onto my finger. He takes the crystal box and slips it into his pocket.

"I'm just going to sort out the payment for our priest. I'll be right back." He leans down and kisses me then walks out of the room towards the reception desk.

I find myself alone.

Standing in a room just inside a chapel in Las Vegas.

To my left I can see the reception desk. Just beyond that is the door that leads out onto the street.

I look down at my dress.

Blinking many times and trying to work out if this is all real.

The ring on my finger is solid enough to be real.

The dress hugging my body feels real.

The panic spinning in my stomach feels real.

But this *can't* be real.

My father will kill me.

But do I care what my father thinks at this point? He wants to send me away. He doesn't even want me around anymore. It doesn't matter to him if I even *exist* anymore. He wants me on the other side of freaking planet.

I look towards the open door, out into the reception area and I watch Rufino talking to the lady behind the counter.

That man wants me.

He wants to marry me. For some crazy, fucked up, wild reason - he wants to marry me *right now* in Vegas.

I'm torn between running out of the door and trying to escape or going the way down this rabbit hole and marrying him.

He's even crazier than I am.

Unless I choose to go through with this. Then I guess we are equally out of our minds.

"Rufino." I hesitate, as he walks back into the room.

"They're ready for us, vixen."

"I - I don't know—"

He grabs my jaw and pulls my face towards his. His eyes are fierce and intense.

"You are marrying me, Verity. This is the only way for us to be together. Now, do you trust me or not?" he growls.

His temper sends sparks of desire shooting through me.

"I trust you." I whisper, my pussy flooding with warmth and my skin tingling.

It's too late now.

I'm too deep in this. No matter which direction I turn in I will be in trouble.

Decide to marry Rufino and be committed to one man for the rest of my life, even though I'm only twenty-three. Or run out of here and go back to my father who will send me away to a convent where I will rot my years away learning how to be a lady.

I could never change who I am.

I never will.

Ultimately, there is no choice.

I have to marry Rufino if he is offering me an escape from everything else.

CHAPTER TWELVE
Rufino

The hesitation in her eyes sparks anger inside me.

I don't think she understands that I'm not giving her a choice in the matter. She will marry me.

She will be mine.

"You are marrying me, Verity. This is the only way for us to be together. Now, do you trust me or not?" I snap at her, not wanting to, but losing my patience. It was hard enough to get her away from those guards and now she wants to toy with me.

"I trust you." She whispers, biting her lip and sending a bolt of desire through my body. The nervous expression in her eyes turns me on. It makes me want to rip her clothes off and take her right here.

"Good. Then do as I say and be a good girl." I take her hand and she follows, tipsy and swaying behind me into the reception area.

"We're ready." I tell the woman behind the desk.

"Aright, just go through there." She points to a big wooden door which is currently being pushed open from the other side.

"Wait. Stop." Verity shouts in horror.

I growl as I turn towards her, ready to throw her over my shoulder and carry her to the alter.

"Verity, I told you to be a good girl." I warn her.

"I need a *veil*." She says her eyes wide with serious concern.

"Oh." I say, looking around.

A drunk couple stumbles through the now open doors and into the reception area.

"Where am I going to get a *veil*?" Verity ask again, sounding even more worried.

The bride of the other couple comes stumbling over to Verity. "Do you want to borrow mine, sweetie?" She slurs her words, hanging onto Verity, giggling as she pulls the sheer white lace loose from her own hair.

"Oh, yes, *please*. Thank you so much." Verity helps her unclip her veil and between the two of them they pin in into Verity's hair.

I grin as I watch her, not able to believe that she is about to become my wife.

When she turns towards me again she is smiling, the veil is sitting to the left. I reach out and straighten it, nodding with satisfaction. "You are beautiful, Verity."

"I know." She says with all the sass I am accustomed to from her.

We walk through the wooden doors together - into a tiny, but very elegant church. The priest greets us with a warm welcome and encourages us to step up to the alter.

My eyes are on her the entire time he is talking.

She looks like an angel.

Those dark red lips and glittering blue eyes, the white dress hugging her waist and tight over her hips. My heart is thrumming a steady beat of excitement at the thought of owning her.

She is about to belong to me in such a meaningful way that she can never leave me.

She will be mine.

Even her father won't have a right to send her away.

No one will have a right to touch my wife.

My wife.

Not a person in the world will question our love for each other.

"Do you, Rufino Vece, take this woman to be your lawfully wedded wife?"

"I do." My stomach tightens with anticipation.

"Do you, Verity A'Vara, take this man to be your lawfully wedded husband?"

She grins, her eyes shining up at me. "I do." She says.

"Well, then there is nothing else to do but this - I now pronounce you husband and wife. You may kiss your bride."

Without wasting a second I step forward, wrap my arms around her and dip her backwards - sealing our words with a passionate kiss.

If the priest wasn't watching us, I would have bent her over the wooden benches and fucked her right here.

She is *mine*.

I *own* her.

"Mr. And Mrs. Vece." the priest says, trying to call for our attention.

I pull her back to her feet, ending the kiss.

The priest gestures for us to leave the church. He's ready for his next couple. His next Vegas wedding.

And I am ready to take my wife somewhere more private.

In the reception area Verity runs over to the other bride and hands her veil back to her. "Thank you so much." She hugs her tightly, almost causing both of them to fall over, then she runs back to me.

"Now what, *husband*?" She giggles, brushing her hand up my chest.

"Now - we celebrate, of course, Mrs. Vece." I pick her up and throw her over my shoulder, carrying her, laughing and screaming, out of the chapel back to my car.

We don't have to drive far at all before I spot a motel.

Those generic bright neon lights, with flashing pink lips and green handcuffs on the side of the building, confirm that it is exactly the type of place I'm looking for.

Somewhere where no one will think to search for us.

Verity is already opening her door when I get there but before she can climb out of the car, I hoist her back over my shoulder.

The sound of her laughter makes me smile.

A smile crept across my face as I realized the level of privacy was even higher than expected.

There isn't even a receptionist.

Verity wiggles so much trying to see what's going on that I set her down in front of me, wrapping my arm around her waist so that we are both facing the computer screen.

All I have to do is select the themed room I want, swipe my credit card, and the key falls into a tray beneath the screen.

It *should* be that simple. I was just going to select the first available option. But the idea of choosing the best room suddenly excited Verity.

She flicks through the options, some making us laugh, some making us questions humans as a species.

"Cowboy theme, tentacle monsters, a rose garden, mermaids, jungle fever, Elvis." she keeps scrolling through a seemingly endless list of images until she gasps in delight.

She scrolls one back and clicks to accept the bondage room.

A girl after my own heart. The more I learn about her the more I fall in love.

I swipe my bank card and as promised the key

card for our room falls into the tray like a vending machine.

Verity grabs it and tries to bolt away, but I'm too quick. Looping my arm around her waist I lift her up against my side as though she was a rag doll. She goes limp, thinking it might make her harder to carry, but she weights nothing to me.

Upon pushing the door of our motel open, we are greeted with a dark room, black walls, and dark silk bedding. There are handcuffs on the walls and hidden red neon lights that give the space an ominous glow.

Verity laughs when I set her down. She runs over to the bed to bend over it. Being cheeky, she wiggles her ass at me. Teasing me. Not knowing that I am already on the verge of tearing her apart.

I've been so fucking hot for her since she said *I do* and became my wife that I almost pulled the car over and had my way with her in the back seat.

I close the door and latch it behind me.

Then I turn to watch her. She's still bent over with her back towards me.

Unbuttoning my shirt and tugging it off my shoulders I admire her while she switches from wiggling her ass to sliding her dress up over her hips and running her hands up the inside of her thighs.

Mine. I think to myself.

My cock is so fuck hard against my pants its aching.

I slide my belt free and snap it in my hands.

She gasps and stands up to glare at me.

When she sees what I'm holding she grins.

"Bend over." I demand, kicking my pants off.

Her eyes drift down to my cock. She licks her lips.

With slight hesitation she does as she's told and bends over the bed again.

I don't give her a chance to change her mind.

Flicking the leather belt I let it lick across her ass cheeks.

Not hard, but hard enough to leave a beautiful red streak on her creamy, smooth skin.

She squeals and spins around with defiance in her eyes.

But I'm on top of her before she can say a word, pushing her onto the bed I grab her legs and drag them apart. Her shoes fall off as she wiggles and tries to escape my grasp.

Her eyes shine with happiness, mirroring my enjoyment.

To my surprise she manages so land a kick against my ribs and slip free of me, moving up towards the top of the bed with a mischievous laugh.

"Naughty girl." I growl, standing on the mattress, grabbing her around the throat and lifting her up against the wall.

My eyes grow dark with satisfaction when I spot the rope hanging from a deadbolt in the wall.

"No - wait." Verity stammers as I grab her wrists and twist the cord around them - she is bound to the wall. And she is all mine.

I spin her around so that her back is facing me.

"You wanted to taunt me with that gorgeous ass of yours, now I am going to take you from behind." I growl against her ear as I push my body against hers, pinning her to the wall.

She pushes her ass out, rubbing it over my cock.

My cock throbs harder and I can't stand another second of this.

Slipping my hands around her lace panties I rip them off with one hard tug. I kick her legs apart and thrust my cock into her tight, pink, beautiful little pussy. *My pussy.* Every part of her belongs to me.

She squeals in delight and collapses against me, her legs almost giving way.

Wrapping my arm around her waist I hold her steady so that I can fuck her as hard as I want to fuck her.

Slamming into her I bury myself deep inside her over and over again.

I can see the rope cutting into her skin and I love the sight of it. Her delicate fingers wrapped around the braided cord and her wedding ring glinting pink in the red light.

She is bound to *me*.

Forever.

I'll never let her leave me.

CHAPTER THIRTEEN
Verity

Rufino stands behind me, his massive bulking body trapping me against the wall. Not that I could move if I wanted to. The rope tied around my wrists is burning against my skin with each thrust of his cock into me.

My pussy is pulsing over him, my legs weak with desire.

He is fucking me as though he owns me.

Like I am something he possesses and can do whatever he wants with.

It's so fucking hot I'm going crazy with desire.

Every time he pushes up into me I cry out in pleasure.

I've never felt this free before.

This wild and naughty.

He locks his hands around my waist.

I arch my back towards him, wanting him to fill me up in every way.

His hand runs up the front of my body and around my jaw, his long fingers dipping into my mouth.

I wrap my lips around them, licking and sucking while his cock plunges into me over and over again.

He growls against my ear and the sound of his pleasure pushes me over the edge. I can't hold back anymore.

My pussy tightens, then throbs and spasm as my orgasm exploded inside me like fireworks, shooting through my entire body.

I moan loudly, collapsing against him, his cock is rock hard inside me and with one last, forceful thrust he releases his own pleasure into me.

We stand against the wall, catching our breath. My heart is racing, and I can't wipe the stupid drunk grin off my face. He leans down and kisses me along my neck, across my shoulder. I sigh in contentment.

Rufino unties the rope from my wrists and I drop to my knees, letting myself collapse onto the bed, my hair floats around me like water over the silky blankets.

He steps over me then lies down next to me.

He pulls me up against his chest and I snuggle into him, realizing that I've only been able to sleep next to him once. I've been dreaming about being with him with no inhibitions, just him and me.

I close my eyes, the world still spinning.

His hand is drifting gently up and down my spine, ticklish, but pleasurable.

I'm too tired to wiggle away.

Tonight was so much fun.

I can't believe I got away from the guards. A soft giggle falls from my lips when I think about my father's face when he finds out.

Rufino reaches up and brushes his hand through my hair.

"Do you want to play some more?" he asks, his voice deep, sounding sleepy as well.

My drunken mind screams *yes* but my exhausted body just snuggles closer against him. "Let me rest for a little bit." I mumble, drifting towards sleep.

Waking up is like opening my eyes into a genuine nightmare. The headache activates with full force and when I swallow my mouth is dry like it is full of cotton balls. This hangover is beyond anything I've ever felt.

Fury coursed through me as I drank last night at the party and since stepping off the plane in Las Vegas.

I groan loudly, almost crying from the pain of my hangover.

"What did I do?" I mumble, reaching up to hold my head still because it feels like it's going to fall off.

"Hello my beautiful wife." His voice makes me jump. "I brought you a coffee, some water, and some headache pills."

"Rufino?" I roll over, towards the sound of his voice, and my head pounds harder. Pain throbs against the walls of my skull and my stomach churns with nausea.

Forcing my eyes open the ache in my body grows worse.

The motel room comes into focus.

Oh no.

Oh no.

Fuck.

No.

"Are we - married?" I mutter through my cotton ball mouth.

"Yes, Mrs. Vece. You are my wife." He sits down on the bed next to me and I close my eyes again.

This is too much.

I've done stupid things. Sure. *Plenty*.

But *I'm only twenty-three years old*. I can't be married.

The bed shifts under his weight as he moves to help me sit up.

"Drink this. I promise it will help. I think you might have had an entire bottle of vodka by yourself last night."

I groan in protest as he sits me up against the pillow and forces a bottle of still water into my hands.

"Open." He demands. I open my mouth and he drops two pills onto my tongue.

"Now drink."

The first tip of water is like rain in the desert. My throat grabs at it and my body begs for more.

The second sip of water is like someone punching me in the stomach. Nausea leaps forward and I have to press my lips together to stop if from coming back up.

"Ugh." I groan again, because it's all I seem to do.

"Sleep a bit more, vixen. I'm right here with you. Give the headache tables some time to kick in."

He doesn't have to ask me twice.

I snuggle back down into the bed and close my eyes.

Restless, pain filled sleep steals me away for a while longer.

My dreams are vivid and confusing. The silky sheets are unfamiliar against my skin.

When I open my eyes, the second time the painkillers have helped. My head doesn't weight a ton and my eyes aren't aching as much. The nausea is down to a dull annoyance.

I drag myself into a sitting position. Rufino is next to me on the bed, reading news articles on his phone.

"I got you a fresh coffee." He grins at me.

"You are amazing. How are you not as hungover as me?" I sigh, picking it up and taking a sip of the heavenly dark liquid.

"I think you drank enough for three people."

I sit quietly for a moment trying to piece my thoughts together. We were both drunk last night otherwise we would never have done something so stupid.

Looking down at my hand I wiggle the finger wearing the beautiful pink ring. It's so pretty.

But I don't want to be married.

I'm sure he doesn't either.

"Rufino - we are going to stop at the chapel and get the wedding annulled right?" I say firmly.

"What?" he snarls at me, his eyes darkening.

"I - I mean - I don't want to break up with you - but marriage is - it's so severe." I stammer, nervous of his intense reaction.

He gets off the bed, standing alongside it and glaring down at me.

"*No*. We will not be annulling the wedding, Verity. You are my wife. You are mine. There is no fucking way I'll be letting you go."

"Rufino I *have* to go. My father will kill us both. I need to be back home before he knows any of this happened. And I *can't be married*."

The pain of my hangover is now being overruled by the panic building in my chest. Rufino looks furious. The disappointment in his eyes is terrifying.

"I'm sorry you feel that way, vixen."

He takes the coffee from my hand and sets it down on the bedside table, then lifts me out of the bed. I'm too stunned to stop him.

Grabbing some rope he wraps it around my wrists, slaps tape over my mouth and carries me out to his car.

I keep thinking - this is a joke - this is a joke. Any second now he's going to put me down.

But he doesn't.

He puts me into the trunk of his car.

I scream against the tape but only a muffled sound comes out.

I kick against the closed trunk and back of the seats, but nothing happens. Rufino doesn't open the trunk laughing and teasing me.

The engine starts.

The car moves.

And my panic sets in for real.

Last night we were playing games - he kidnapped

me, and we did some wild stupid and fun things - but this - *this* is too much.

This is too real.

Now that the fun glowing haze of alcohol has worn off all I'm left with is the truth.

Last night was only a game to *me*.

He planned every piece of that evening down to the last moment. He knew he was going to marry me before he even got to Las Vegas. He *knew* he was going to kidnap me and make me his wife.

But why?

I don't get it.

Why did he go to such extremes?

We drive for about twenty minutes and I end up just closing my eyes and focusing on my breathing, forcing myself to be as calm as possible and to ignore the throbbing ache of my hangover headache which is now back with a vengeance.

Gravel crunches beneath the tires as we slow down and then come to a complete stop. A car door opens, then closes, and his footsteps crunch against gravel as well. My heart is racing in anger when he opens the trunk.

I curse him from beneath the tape over my mouth. Shooting insults with my eyes, letting him see how furious I am.

Rufino lifts me out of the trunk and sets me down on the gravel. It bites into my bare feet.

"I'm going to take the tape off now. It might hurt a little."

I narrow my eyes, breathing heavily.

He pulls the tape off in one quick movement and I scream at full volume. Not from the pain of the tape peeling off my skin but from pure anger and adrenalin.

"What the fuck is going on?" I shout, stomping my foot, then regretting it as more stones bite against my skin.

"Verity, take a deep breath and calm down."

"I won't calm down. Don't tell me to calm down. You put me in the trunk of your car. I don't have to *calm down*."

The scorching desert sun is backing down on me and I squish my eyes closed, wanting to vomit again. Maybe, for my *sake*, I should calm down.

"I'm going to untie your hands." He says, turning me around so that he can pull the rope off.

As soon as my hands are free I take off, running at full speed.

My feet hurt, my head hurts, I want to vomit, I'm thirsty and in pain.

So, I stop running and turn to look at him.

That asshole is leaning again the side of the car with his arms folded across his chest.

"You aren't even trying to chase me." I huff, shouting over the short distance I put between us.

"Where are you planning on going? You're in a desert with no shoes in a little white dress."

I huff louder and spin away from him, even more determined to get away now.

I walk down the road with no idea of where it leads.

Behind me I hear the car start. He drives until he is alongside me, moving forward at the same pace as my walking.

"Go away." I snap.

"Just get in the car, my love. We can go home."

"Home? Or home? Where is home?"

"My home. You're my wife and you belong in my home."

"Is that so?" I sass, walking faster.

"For fuck sakes." He mutters, pulling the hand break up the climb out, marches over to me, drags me to the car and throws me into the passenger seat - slamming the door closed.

I sit with my arms folded across my chest and my lower lip pouted out, my face turned away from him.

Driving is better than walking though.

No one should subject themselves to a desert stroll with a headache like this.

Rufino drives us to the airport and I don't bother fighting as he leads me onto his private jet. I'm tired. I want food. I want to sleep. I will deal with this stuff-up of a situation when I'm better.

CHAPTER FOURTEEN
Rufino

On the jet Verity is sulky and quiet. It's not a long flight, but I do my best to make her comfortable. I arrange for her to be served a massive burger and crispy fries. The best food for a hangover which she is suffering from. She eats in silence but enjoys it.

She is refusing to look in my direction - as defiant as ever.

I notice with amusement though that she's still wearing the wedding ring. I half expected her to throw it at me by now with the way she is carrying on about everything. Earlier on I even caught her looking at it and turning it on her finger. That slight gesture gives me hope that she'll relax and accept this for what it is.

She has no choice about the marriage. It's already done.

She can fight this as much as she wants. I'm not ending our marriage.

She is my wife.

We arrive at my second mansion just outside the city. The one I use when I need some time alone, away from people and especially my brothers.

She sighs loudly when she climbs out of the car, reminding me she's mad at me.

I slip my arm around her waist walking up the steps towards the front door. She doesn't push me away. If she was that angry with me she would have shoved my hand away right away.

I see it as a good sign.

She has a right to be angry, anyway. I locked her in the trunk of my car to drive her out of Las Vegas without causing too much of a scene. I couldn't have her sitting on the front seat trying to open the door and roll out or something ridiculous like that - something I one hundred percent would expect from her.

She steps into my home, which is now her home too.

I close and lock the door behind us.

"The entire place is a fortress, my love. You are free to escape - but I assure you it won't be possible."

"We'll see about that." She hisses, then marches up the stairs. "Where can I find a shower?" She blurts out, glaring over her shoulder at me.

"Second room on the right. You'll also find a full closet of clothing in your size."

Her mouth drops open. "How long have you been planning this, Red?"

Cute. She called me by my nickname. That means she's still into me.

I grin.

"Since you told me your father had booked your flight to Europe."

Verity blinks several times in quick succession. Her mouth still hanging open in shock. Then she shakes her head and storms away.

I better give her some time to herself. At least, now that we're home, I don't have to worry about her going anywhere.

The next few days test my patience in ways I never imagined were possible.

Verity is a nightmare.

She's like a little demon temptress running wild in my house.

She fights with me, provoking me every chance she gets. And she's damn good at it. She knows what she's doing.

Then she taunts me with her body and makes me forget why I was getting angry in the first place.

Every conversation is around the fact that I forced her to marry me and I am now holding her prisoner and not letting her live her life. She doesn't seem to get that the moment I let her go - her father is going to send her away. She should appreciate what I've done for her - not be fighting me on it.

I'm standing in front of the coffee machine, waiting for it to finish making my cappuccino. It's late, and I've already had too many of these today, but I need one more. I'll call it a coping mechanism. The caffeine helping me stay a little sharper to deal with this new challenge.

"You tricked me. You forced me to marry you." She snaps.

I turn to face her, my fists clenched at my side.

"I didn't force you to do anything. No one held a gun to your head." I snarl, glaring down at her. She is standing with her hands on her hips and that look on her face that confuses the hell out of me because it annoys me and turns me on at the same time.

Her little nose is scrunched up and her lips are pouted out as she throws me a look of pure thunder. They always told me dynamite comes in small packages. But Verity is more like a nuclear weapon waiting to detonate in my life.

"You didn't even *ask me*. And - and - *and* I *was* so drunk. I was in no state to be making important decisions that affect the *rest of my life.*"

"And and and." I roll my eyes.

"Don't roll your eyes at me." She punches my arm.

I chuckle and her eyes flare darker.

"You'll have to do better than that." I smirk.

She shoves both of her hands hard against my chest and tries to push me, but I don't budge an inch.

"Ugh." She huffs, stomping her foot. "You're so annoying."

"And you're so little." I tease her making the situation worse.

She tries to push me again but this time I grab her wrists and lift her onto the kitchen counter. She squeals when I push her legs apart and stand with my hips between them, grabbing her ass and pulling her right up against me.

"I didn't see you complaining on our wedding night." I whisper against her ear and she digs her nails into my back.

"This is cheating." She says breathlessly.

I sigh, my body yearning for her and wanting to share that with her, not all of this heated tension. I hate the fact that we've been doing nothing but fight since she got here.

I lean back to look into her eyes.

"Verity, don't resist me." Those eyes of hers sending shivers down my spine and haunting thoughts through my body.

"Then let me go." She whispers in response. The complete opposite of what I want to hear.

A low growl rumbles from my chest and my jaw muscles feather in agitation.

"I will *never* let you go. When will you accept that?" I snarl.

She pushes me away again and I step back, utterly exhausted by the looping conversations.

"Why did you have to *marry* me, Rufino? What was the point of it?" she moans. "You could have just kidnapped me without all the rings and commitment and things."

She's still wearing it. Despite all of her protests - she *is* still wearing it.

I reach up and take her hand, looking at how beautiful the ring looks against her skin.

Bound to me.

How can she not understand? I've tried to explain it before but she wasn't listening. She's like that when she's angry. I don't think she hears a work I say to her. But I'll keep telling her repeatedly until she hears me.

"Because now that we are *married* no one can take you from me. No one would dare. You are my wife and I decide what happens to you. Without my permission your father can never send you to Europe."

"*You* decide? What - like you *own* me?" She says in anger.

I move close to her again, my face inches from hers. "Correct. I do own you, Verity Vece."

"*No one owns me.*" She shouts.

She kicks away from the kitchen counter and storms out. I hear her marching up the stairs and it sounds like she's crying which crushes me.

For a moment I stand with my eyes closed and my hands pressed against the counter, my head hanging low in defeat.

Dammit.

This is not going how I planned for any of this to go down. I assumed she would be overjoyed to be living here with me. At least once she got over the fact that I put her in the trunk of my car.

But she's fixated on the trap of marriage, as she keeps referring to it.

Trapped.

I understand her frustration. It's not like I wanted to rush into marriage either. It's so official, so final. *But I want her.* I want to be with her, and this was the best way I could achieve that.

The risk of losing her was greater than my fear of marriage.

The reality of her emotions sinks in.

She believes I've clipped her wings.

Perhaps I have in a way.

But it's *not* in the way she thinks. I never want her to change or stop being her wild self. That's what I love about her.

That spontaneous unpredictable girl I met in the club.

I sip my coffee, letting time slip away, giving her space to calm down before I make my way upstairs. I pause, listening to figure out if she's still angry.

I push the bedroom door open and step inside.

She is lying face down on the bed, her shoulders are shaking with tears that are still falling.

I sigh and sit down next to her, pulling her into my arms.

"Vixen, you're right."

She huffs.

I stroke my hand over her hair and hold her tighter against my body.

"You're right - no one owns you, not like *that*."

She says nothing, but I can feel her relaxing in my

arms. She's not fighting me or pushing me away which is a good sign.

"I did what I thought was right - so that you and I could be together."

I whisper, as though I am trying to calm a wild horse, my voice is soothing, and my hands are moving gently over her.

"I never wanted to lose you - the thought of you going to Europe - I couldn't let that happen."

Verity isn't crying anymore.

I hear her take a deep breath.

"I know." She says, her words muffled against my chest.

"What do you know?" I ask, leaning her away from me so that I can see her face. She scowls at me and buries her face into my chest again. I chuckle.

"What do you know, vixen?" I ask again.

"I don't want to go anywhere without you either." She confesses and my heart melts at her words.

"So, then we can make this work. Stop being so full of attitude all the time." I laugh, teasing her.

"Attitude? You're holding me prisoner - what else am I supposed to do?" She snaps.

Fuck.

I always say the wrong thing.

She shifts away from me and folds her arms across her chest, determined not to make eye contact with me.

After staring at her for a while I grin, knowing how to fix this.

"Are you hungry?" I ask.

I watch her eyes sneak a peek towards me.

"Chinese?" I say, still grinning.

No response.

"Pizza?"

Her eyes drift towards me again.

"Sushi?"

She bites her lip.

"Sushi. Mm. Ok. I can make that happen. Let me go downstairs and order some. Why don't you hop in the shower, the hot water will help you relax. Then get into those comfy pink sweatpants you look so cute in and by the time you come downstairs the food will be here."

"And a movie." She demands, trying to hide her smile.

"And a movie. I'll pick one for us. Netflix and sushi. It sounds like a perfect evening with you."

CHAPTER FIFTEEN
Verity

One moment I feel as though things are going to be ok - and then next we are back at each other's throats.

I'm going crazy.

I don't know how much more of this I can take.

I don't want to fight with Red, but he's not understanding me. He doesn't get it. He doesn't understand the intensity of my anger towards him.

I sigh, sitting on the edge of the second last step of the long staircase that leads upstairs.

Maybe if I could find a different way to explain it to him.

If I could make him see it from my point of view.

What is my point of view?

It's about him marrying me —

"Dammit." I shout, standing up suddenly and marching back and forth in the foyer.

I've been looping with these damn thoughts for so long now that I don't even think I can put them into words anymore.

All I am sure of, is that I'm angry.

Angry because I'm married?

Yes, sure.

Angry because he forced me to marry him?

No, not quite. Because even though I was drunk he *didn't* force me - did he? I guess I can't answer that because I didn't put much effort into trying *not* to get married on that night.

So, then I'm angry because I'm a prisoner here.

That's it.

Although - if I left, my father would ship me off to

Europe, and I'd be a prisoner in a far worse situation.

"Fuck." I say, hearing my voice echo against the high ceilings.

If I'm really honest with myself, then none of this is his fault - but at the same time all if it is his fault.

If I hadn't met Rufino Vece, I would just be carrying on with my life the way I always have been. Partying with my friends. Having fun. Without a care in the world.

Is that what I want?

The same monotonous thing over and over again. Because that's what was happening. I was already getting bored with parties. I'd push the limits, craving something more.

Craving him.

Maybe - I got exactly what I asked for.

"Are you going to pace up and down the foyer all day?" He asks, leaning against the wall with his arms folded over his broad chest.

"If you let me go I could pace up and down the mall instead?" I say mockingly.

"Verity - please don't start." He sighs heavily.

"Start what? Complaining that I'm not even allowed outside? People need sunshine to survive. It's a fact. You are murdering me by not letting me go outside and feel the sun on my skin. Vitamin D is a real thing."

He rolls his eyes.

"Alright, I'm murdering you. I'm the worst person in the world. I get it."

"Well, that's the first thing you've said since I got here that sounds true."

"Ugh." He huffs. "I am so fucking over this. Maybe I will let you go. Is that what you want? To walk out of this door. To go back to your father?"

My stomach twists into the tightest knot and my heart stalls in my rib cage. What if he kicked me out and force me to go home?

Fuck.

The fear running through me becomes ominous and dark.

Then the truth slams into me like a brick wall.

A hundred miles an hour.

I wouldn't leave even if he let me.

But what if he didn't give me a choice?

Fuck.

"That's not the point. This whole mess is your fault." I snarl, desperate to change the subject.

"My fault?" He says in exasperation. "You walked up to me in the club that night - in case you don't remember - you kissed me."

"And you could have left it at that. You didn't have to invite me home with you afterwards."

"You didn't have to come home with me afterwards." He shouts.

"You didn't have to make me marry you." I yell back at him.

"Oh here we go again." He throws his hands in the air in annoyance.

I don't want to look at him right now because all I want to do is slap him. I'm so angry I don't know where to direct it or how to deal with it.

I storm from the foyer and march into the living room.

But he follows me.

"When are you going to stop blaming me and start taking some responsibility for the role you played in all of this, Verity?"

"Leave me alone." I snap.

"No." He replies defiantly.

"Leave. Me. Alone." I shout, picking up a pillow from the sofa and throwing it at him.

He catches it mid air and storms towards me, taking long terrifying strides.

He lifts me off my feet and throws me onto the sofa, pinning me down with his body.

"If you want to play rough we can play rough, fire cracker."

He's got my arms pinned behind my back, so I lift my head and bite him on the shoulder.

"Ow." He yells grabbing my throat and pushing my head back into the sofa.

I cry out, kick my legs, and Rufino positions himself so that my legs wrap around his hips.

I can feel how hard his cock is - pressing against my pussy.

My heart races a million miles an hour.

He pushes harder against me, rubbing himself between my legs.

I spread my legs open wider and lift my hips towards him. Adrenaline from anger quickly turns to fiery desire.

Rufino leans close to my face and presses his lips against mine.

The kiss sends sharp bolts of electricity shooting through my body.

Out of nowhere, we are tearing clothes off each other in desperation to be skin on skin. I want his body on mine. I want to be as close to him as possible.

He wraps his arm around the back of my hips and lifts my pussy up towards him.

When his cock slides into me I gasp with pleasure.

He moves slow but pushes deep into me. The undulating dance of his hips thrusting his cock inside me and making my body shudder as I let go of my anger and give myself to him.

His cock stretches me open and throbs inside me.

I wouldn't leave him.

He could hand me the keys to his car and open the front door for me - I wouldn't leave him.

Rufino speeds up, pushing his hips faster and harder, grunting with effort every time he slams into me.

The soft moans that are falling from my lips seem to make him harder, more excited.

I scratch my nails over his biceps, down his arm and he spreads his fingers wide, threading them through mine he pins my hand above my head.

My legs shake, and he grabs my ankle and lifts it above his shoulder, folding me so that he can push deeper into me.

It is my final undoing.

My pussy clamps tightly over his cock and I come all over him.

He explodes inside me with a low growl and a hard thrust, closing his eyes for a moment and breathing heavily.

Red lies down on top of me, his head resting on the pillow next to mine. Then he rolls and pulls me with him, onto his chest.

Neither of us speaks.

Our breathing is synchronized. I am at peace here with him in this moment and for the life of me I can't figure out why we've been fighting the entire time.

I sigh softly, wanting to share my heart with him but knowing that the moment I open my mouth I'm going to say the wrong thing and we'll end up in another argument.

He strokes his hand down the back of my head, his fingers brushing through my hair.

He sighs as well.

How can it be that we are feeling the same things but unable to express them to each other?

We are so alike in so many ways it's confusing.

"My love." He whispers.

"Mm?"

He takes a deep breath, choosing his words carefully as I would want to choose mine.

"This whole situation is not ideal. It's not the most perfect way we could have started our journey together - the marriage - it - um - it scares me too. But it's only a small part of everything else. The most important thing - and maybe the only things that matters in all of this - is that I want to be with you, Verity. I can't lose you. It all happened so fast. I fell hard. My heart never wants to let you go. That's what matters."

I listen. Not interrupting or telling him he's wrong for a change.

I just wait, taking in his words and then thinking them through to understand them.

He continues to stroke his fingers through my hair while I lie with my head on his chest.

I soak in his scent, his warmth, his energy.

Finally, when he might be close to thinking I will never reply, I prop myself up with my chin resting on fingers.

"We've been idiots." I smile softly.

He grins.

"We have been idiots." He nods.

"I want to be with your too, Red. I got freaked out about the whole being married thing. I focused on it too much and didn't step back and look at the complete picture. Or I did - but I was too angry to accept it. I understand why you married me. And it makes sense."

I see the half smirk creeping onto his lips.

I shake my head at him. "If you *dare* say 'I told you so' you are going to be in so much trouble."

"I wouldn't dream of it." He chuckles, still fighting to hide the giant smirk or triumph.

Wiggle closer to his face I press my lips against his, then whisper "Can we start over? Pretend like you are just bringing me home for the first time?"

Out of nowhere he sits up, with his arms wrapped around me he lifts me right off the sofa and carries me to the front door. He pulls the handle down and kicks it open then steps out onto the front step.

He sets me down next to him.

We are both buck naked standing at the door, and I can't stop laughing.

He pushes the door open from the outside and gestures for me to go in. "Welcome to your home, our home. Let me give you a tour. You are going to especially love the custom rain storm shower I had installed and the high end coffee machine."

I am laughing so hard I can barely walk straight.

"Is there a heated pool?" I ask, encouraging his games.

"And a jacuzzi and out back we have a state-of-the-art sauna and an air-conditioned sun room with a gym."

"Are you kidding me - all this time there was a gym? If I don't work out I go a little crazy?" I laugh.

"Wow - I wish you'd told me that earlier. We could have avoided all of this drama." He scoops me up into his arms and wraps my legs around his waist.

I giggle as he presses his lips against mine.

"We both aren't the type of people who would have chosen marriage, because we are both such free spirits. But *I love you,* Verity and I know you love me too. So, we can make this work."

I run my fingers up the back of his thick neck, threading them through his dark red hair. "We can make this work. I'm sorry I was difficult." I smile, kissing him again.

"I really love your bad attitude." He grins.

"You really shouldn't encourage me." I giggle.

CHAPTER SIXTEEN
Rufino

Finally, we have found our way back to each other and things are going perfectly between us. This is what I dreamed of. This is what I wanted us to be.

The last two days have been pure bliss.

Verity and I are back to our normal selves. Laughing, teasing each other and joking around. We also can't keep our hands off each other.

We have to figure things out soon. We can't hide in this mansion forever. But we needed these few days of celebration and comfort to enjoy each other after working out our personal issues.

It's been so stressful, but now, we are no longer questioning our choice to be together - only how to deal with everyone else. All of those people who believe they have a say in how we live *our* lives.

My phone has been on silent all morning, my full attention on my wife because she deserves nothing less. In a quiet moment, while we are realign on the sofa, I glance at it to make sure the world isn't falling apart out there - I groan loudly, instantly regretting my decision. Because, if my brothers anger is anything to go by, the world *is* in fact falling apart and it's my fault.

"What's wrong?" Verity asks, stretching her legs out on the sofa and putting them on my lap.

I run my hand up and down her smooth skin while I read his messages.

"You're all over the news again. Your father released an article about your kidnapping. He's hunting for you and offering a reward for anyone who has information. He says he will leave no stone unturned and all of that type of bullshit."

"We knew that would happen." She scrunches her nose.

"We did - but that's not why I'm groaning. It's because my brothers figured I took you. They are raging."

Verity sits up, looking worried. "Will they tell my father?" She asks. "If he finds out it was you—" her words trail off as her throat tightens with stress.

"I wish I could say no with confidence, but anything is possible when it comes to my brothers. They might throw me to the wolves to save themselves." I shrug, wrapping my hand around her delicate foot and pressing my fingers into her sole.

"But they're your family." She says, confused.

"Yes, and I put them in a lot of danger by choosing you over them. They will want to protect their own wives and children. I wouldn't really blame them if they gave me up. I also wouldn't put it past them."

"How can we stay ahead of this?"

I bite the inside of my cheek, staring at my phone while I think.

Staying ahead of this is exactly what we need to do.

My thoughts are churning, looking for a solution.

The same idea keeps popping up in my mind. An idea I have had a few times over the past two days, but I kept pushing aside.

Maybe it's what we need to do.

"Red? What are you thinking? I know that look."

I turn towards my beautiful wife and grin.

"We give ourselves up." I say, nodding enthusiastically and squeezing her leg.

"Give ourselves up?" she already looks like she doesn't like this idea. "No, that's a terrible idea, Rufino." She pulls her legs off my lap and sits up dead straight. Her shoulders tense and her body rigid with stress.

"It's the perfect idea, my love. We do it *boldly*. We announce our marriage in an exclusive interview - let the world see we are together, and we are in love. If we make a public scene about it, then your father can't go overboard with his retaliation because that will also be in the public eye."

She narrows her eyes at me and tilts her head to the side.

"Oh. Wow. That's actually brilliant." She says, scrunching her nose as she considers the full plan. "It might just work."

Grab her face in my hands and kiss her hard. She laughs when I pull away.

"I better make some phone calls then. The sooner we do this the better."

Choosing to face my battles one at a time I ignore my brother's messages and open my contacts to find the man I really need to talk to.

Jake Blanch.

The phone rings one before he answers.

"Red, my man. Tell me you have something juicy for me." He laughs that loud rolling laughter I'm accustomed to.

"The most juicy story you'll get all month."

"That's a big promise. This month has been rather exciting already. Big mafia boss's daughter got herself kidnapped, and that's the main talk of the town - can you top that?"

I chuckle. "Oh, I can top it alright. In fact I can blow it right out of the water. I'm sending you an address. Come over this afternoon. I'll give you an exclusive."

"Hang on a second - *A'Vara* - that's the girl you were caught hooking up with. Is this about her? Do you know what happened to her?" the puzzle pieces click in his mind and rich excitement floods from him.

"I'll see you this afternoon. Bring your photographer."

♥

The photograph they take of us is stunning.

Verity is wearing a long, flowing white dress symbolic of our announcement. We stand together in front of the massive stone and steel archway that curves over the pool. A dramatic piece of architecture that looks bold and strong.

Verity is leaning against me with her hand on my chest, kissing me. The stance is very similar to the first photograph that was ever released of us in the media. Of course, that was a purposeful choice. A deliberate jab at those who questioned the authenticity of our relationship.

The article hits the afternoon print and splashes across the front page of every media site. Our images flood social media, and in no time at all, my phone is ringing off the hook.

My brothers are even angrier than before.

I suck it up, the consequences of putting the news out there are inevitable, I answer Masaccio's call, standing outside on the patio watching the wind ripple across the turquoise surface of our pool.

"What the fuck is fucking wrong with you?" he screams into the phone.

"So, no congratulations then?"

"You fucking idiot you've started a war. Her father is going full force with the threats. He's demanding she come home and that a divorce be filed."

"Interesting. I haven't heard from him."

"Because you never answer your phone you fucking selfish asshole."

"You would expect the guy to want to talk to his new son-in-law."

"I'm going to kill you." He blurts out.

"Ye, ye, listen. Can you give her father a message for me?"

"Fuck off, you inconsiderate prick. I'm not your errand boy. But if you don't give his daughter back to him, I will come down there myself and rip her from your hands to return her to where she belongs."

"She belongs with me." I snarl.

"She belongs with her father. Our families are enemies."

I slam the phone down, agitated and pacing faster.

"Who was that?" her voice makes me pause.

"My brother."

"What did he say?"

"He's still angry. your father has been threatening my family."

Verity sighs. "I don't want anyone to get hurt because of us." She says, walking towards me and wrapping her arms around my waist.

"No one is going to get hurt, sweet thing."

"You can't promise me that. You do not know what my father is capable of."

I know what her father is capable of. If you know our world you understand how dark it can get.

Still in my hand my phone rings again.

"Masaccio—" I complain, but when I look down at the screen, I see it's not him. An unknown number. Someone not in my contact list.

I answer, pressing the phone against my ear.

"Who is this?"

"Where the fuck is my daughter, Rufino Vece?"

"Good evening, Luca A'Vara. It's nice to speak to you. I understand you've been speaking to my brothers."

"Where the fuck is Verity?"

"My wife? She's home with me. Where she belongs."

"She's not your fucking wife. There is no way in hell that marriage is legit."

"It's legitimate. I can have a framed copy of the marriage certificate sent over to you if you like."

"You can't be so arrogant that you think I would just let you get away with this?" he snarls.

I glance at Verity who is chewing at her nails, her eyes glassy with anxiety as she shifts from foot to foot, watching me and only hearing half of the conversation.

I move the phone from my ear and press the loud speaker button so that she can hear everything. She has a right to know exactly what is going on. I have no intention of hiding anything from her.

Her father takes a heavy breath on the other side of the phone.

"I called to negotiate." He says.

"Negotiate?"

"Yes, for the return of my daughter. I can have seven million transferred to your account within the hour if you agree to send her back to me."

"Seven million?"

Verity bites so hard into her lip I'm worried she is going to draw blood.

"Yes, I assume it's enough? You are a businessman. I imagine you are as fascinated with money as you with conquering women? On acceptance of the agreement you would be required to divorce my daughter and send her home."

I chuckle. A dark, malicious laugh that is tainted with amusement.

I look at my wife when I answer him.

"The problem, Mr. A'Vara, is that Verity is like no women I have ever met. She is priceless. She is too rare and precious to put any amount on. No, I am not interested in your money. The only thing I want - well, I already have it."

Her eyes are shining, wide, blue orbs of relief. If she thought for even a second that I would give her up for all the money in the world she is mistaken.

She is mine.

Verity is the type of jewel you can't buy. No matter what he offered in trade I would be losing if I gave her up.

For a long moment her father is silent.

I think the line has been disconnected until all hell breaks loose on his end.

He is screaming, raging, throwing a tantrum of monumental proportions.

I wait, watching Verity.

She was relieved when I didn't accept his offer, but now she looks miserable again. She's chewing at her lip and fidgeting with her hands.

When she starts to pace up and down with her head turned to the ground, I worry.

"Verity?" I whisper, so that her father can't hear.

"You don't know what he's capable of." She whimpers.

She's terrified.

"I told you - it doesn't matter. We can get through it. I won't let him take you."

"But is it really worth it?" she is crying now. Silent tears drifting down her cheeks.

"Are you listening to me?" Luca shouts.

"I'm here. I'm listening."

"Where is she? I want to talk to her. Put my daughter on the phone."

"You're on speaker, Mr. A'Vara. Verity has been listening to everything."

He snarls.

"Verity you come home. What the fuck do you think you are playing at? It's obvious you only did this to piss me off. Now the game is over. Come home."

She is still biting her lip.

Her eyes lift and meet mine.

My heart tightens when I speak to her, loud enough so that her father can listen in.

"Verity, if you want to go home you can leave. But I will not, ever, divorce you."

I can feel the tension in the air as both her father and I wait for her answer.

CHAPTER SEVENTEEN
Verity

Rufino is staring at me with an intensity that chills me right to my bones.

Giving me permission to go home would not have been easy for him.

I know he doesn't want me to leave.

But - he gave me a *choice*. Something I have not been given too often in my life. A choice to choose what *I* want. For whatever reason. Without explanation. He is letting me decide my future.

For that - I love him even more. Drawn to him like a moth to a flame.

"Verity." My father snaps over the loud speaker of Rufino's phone.

"Verity, listen to the man. Pack your things. I will have a car collect you within the hour. Tell me where I can send them."

My eyes close for a moment. I take a deep breath.

My father's response is so typical of him.

First, he isn't *asking* anything - he's just flat out *telling* me what is going to happen. *He* hasn't given me any choice in the matter. It's his needs and his wants regardless of the fact that I am my own person.

Second, he isn't even coming to fetch me himself. He wants to send someone else. He doesn't *miss* me. He's not doing this because he can't wait to see me or because he's been worried sick that I was missing. He doesn't love me. I'm not even sure he cares about me at all.

I am a possession that was taken from him and he wants me returned.

This is all to appease his ego. To regain his control over me.

I open my eyes, drawing from the strength that Rufino gives me with his love.

I'm done with the way my father treats me. I'm over his narcissistic bullshit. This is *my* life. I get to say what happens from here on out.

With a surge of adrenalin, panic, and anxiety bolting through me - I take another deep breath and answer.

"No." I say, simple and blunt. As clear as possible. My voice just became a weapon against the years of living beneath my father's strict rules.

"No?" he stammers into the phone. "Don't you dare so no to me. Where the fuck are you? I am sending the driver now."

"No, dad. I choose Rufino. I am staying here. I will not be coming back to your home. That isn't where I live anymore."

Rufino's eyes are locked onto me and that gorgeous smiles of his is making me smile. My heart is swelling with confidence.

"How dare you do this to me? How dare you do this to our family? You have tainted our family name by marrying that scum. You will pay for this. I will tear them apart. I will destroy everything they have ever loved."

"What about what I love, dad? What about what makes me happy? Do you even care? Are you so blinded by your own selfish demands that you can't see that I have a right to choose?" I snap, heating with anger.

"You have no rights. You are *my* daughter until the day I die. I choose for you."

I sigh.

"Not anymore, dad. My husband overrules your choices now. My life is with him."

My father laughs, and it sends an icy shiver up my spine. I shudder and swallow hard, trying to shake off the horrible sensation.

"You will regret this, Verity. When your husband sees what I have in store for him, he will beg me to take you away."

Rufino shakes his head. "It will never happen, Luca. She has made her choice. Be man enough to respect that."

"Man enough? You fucking fool. I am going to kill you. I'm going to burn you to the ground."

Rufino clicks the red button, and the line goes silent.

I want to throw up.

My stomach is churning like a washing machine and my legs are shaking I think I might collapse.

I stumble, grabbing the arm of the nearest chair I sit down.

Tears threaten to spill from my eyes again and I fight against them.

Crying won't help you now, Verity.

The rollercoaster of emotions I've been on, in such a short time during that conversation are now in one single channel. Fear.

You wanted to go against your father - well - good job because now you've provoked him to where he wants to kill the man you love and it's your fault.

My breathing becomes faster and heavier as panic sets in.

Rufino strides towards me. "Hey, breathe Verity, breathe." He grabs me into his arms and holds me tight. "Just breathe. You don't have to be worried about him. He can't touch me."

"He can." I shout, pushing him away. "He can and he will. I *told* you - you don't know what he's capable of. Do you think I want to see you hurt? I can't - Rufino - I can't handle the idea of losing you." I'm sobbing now, my words muffled by the thick lump in my throat and my eyes are blurry with salty streams of tears.

"Stop that." He grabs my shoulders, forcing me to look at him. "Nothing is going to happen to me. And nothing is going to happen to you either. Your father has no power over you, Verity."

He sounds so sure of himself. I wish I could be as confident, but I'm not.

Standing up I know I have to move. I have to walk or run or scream. The build up inside me is too much. I have to let it out.

Anything to release the growing fear.

I take a step away from Rufino.

"Come on, my love, talk to me." He begs.

I shake my head. "No, I need space."

He sighs when I walk away, but I can't focus on that now.

I have to figure out a way to fix what I've done.

I've made a mistake by defying my father like this.

I want to appease him - but I don't want to leave Rufino.

How can I do both?

Is it even possible?

I walk around the entire garden, moving fast, looking down at my feet - thinking - thinking - thinking. Ideas churning and being tossed away, useless. My father is a monster. Capable of monstrous things. I've always known that.

Fear clouds my thoughts.

One singular, constant looping idea. *You've made a mistake. Your father will kill him. It will be your fault.*

Rufino knows me well enough to give me space right now.

If he tried to talk to me in this state, I would just end up fighting with him and I'm so tired of fighting.

I walk around the garden for over an hour.

Thinking about my father, my options, and how I got us all into this mess.

The sun is sinking low on the horizon and the time splashes dark orange streaks across the sky my mind is clear enough to go back into the house.

Or I'm just too tired to think anymore. The adrenalin is depleted and now I'm an empty shell of anxiety.

The evening air is biting cold against my skin and as soon I walk through the patio doors into the living room, Rufino is there, wrapping a jacket over my shoulders.

"I was just about to come out and give this to you." He says, dragging me right up against his body and holding me in such a way that I can't push him from me even if I wanted to.

I don't want to though. Resting my cheek against his chest I lean into him, enjoying the warmth and the comfort of his arms wrapped around me. When he holds me, I can imagine that nothing will ever happen.

I wish he could hold me forever.

"Dinner is ready. Roast chicken and sweet potatoes with mushroom sauce."

"Thanks." I whisper.

We sit in the living room in silence because I'm too tired to speak.

My body is so tense I'm struggling to finish my food. Rufino only dished up a small amount for me but it's still too much.

"I'm going to bed, if that's ok." I mumble.

"Of course, it is. Do you want me to run you a hot bath?"

I look up at him, wondering where he gets the patience to deal with me. My father used to remind me I was a burden and an annoyance - that he wanted to send me away because he could handle me.

Rufino is fighting to keep me at his side.

It's confusing.

My mind keeps taunting me and trying to tell me it's fake somehow. That maybe he has an ulterior motive. Why would someone put themselves at risk like this for me?

Just me.

What if he gets bored with me and all the drama that seems to follow me everywhere? I'm careless. My father has said it a thousand times.

"Verity?"

"A bath would be lovely, thank you."

"I'll get it ready for you now." He says, standing up. He kisses the top of my head before he leaves. My heart melts for him.

I really love him.

I wish I was certain about how this all ends.

After soaking in a hot bubble bath, sprinkled with dried rose petals and lavender and ylang ylang oil I am so relaxed that I can't think. Which is amazing.

Rufino pulls the bed covers back so that I can climb underneath them and snuggle up against him. He wraps his arm around my waist and pulls me close, holding me.

"Rest, my love. Tomorrow is a new day, and we'll figure it all out - I promise. No matter what happens it's you and me together."

I close my eyes and the world sinks away from me.

My father is holding a gun to Rufino's head, and I am blinded with rage and fear.

"Let him go." I scream.

"You should have made a different choice." My father snarls at me.

Behind him a dark shadow is rising like thick black smoke. It creeps forward, dragging the room into darkness.

"Rufino." I scream, fighting to get to him. But the shadow becomes thick and oil and I can't breathe. I can't speak anymore. It pours into my throat and I'm lying on the ground choking for air.

My father's laughter comes from somewhere in the black ooze that's drowning me.

"You should have made a different choice." He says again and a gunshot fires, snapping through the air and making my body jolt with fright.

"Red." His name is stuck in my throat, tight and locked away.

I crawl along the ground and my hands are sticky. When

I look down at them, I see that blood has covered them. Blood that rises up around me.

"Red."

But I know he's gone. Somewhere in the back of my mind I know he's not in the world anymore.

I wake with a fright, bolting up in bed I fight against the blankets that are tangled around my legs. I kick and scream and gasp for air.

Something grabs me and I turn to fight that too - but its Rufino.

He grabs my wrists and pins me down to stop me from lashing out.

"It was a nightmare, Verity. It's me, it's ok." He says.

I blink against the dark room and take several deep breaths.

"You were gone." I shudder at the memory.

"I'm right here."

"But you were gone." I whimper, choking back the tears.

He pulls the blankets lose from around me and readjusts them, then holds me, rocking me until I drift off to sleep again.

I don't have another nightmare, but the memory of the first one won't leave me alone. Even when I wake up the next morning, my chest is tight with fear.

CHAPTER EIGHTEEN
Rufino

My phone blares early in the morning and I sigh, rubbing my hands across my face to wipe the sleep away before I answer it. Who would call at this time?

I reach over and grab the phone, flicking it to answer the call.

"Hello." I mumble, my voice rough and deep.

A quick glance at the screen tells me Masaccio is on the other side of this call. If I'd paid attention and looked before I answered I would have let it go to voicemail.

"Luca A'Vara launched an attack on one of our warehouse last night. He killed three of our security men. I'm done with this bullshit. This ends today, Red. I have spoken to Tuomo and Celso and we all agree - she is going back to her father."

All remnants of sleep disappear in an instant as anger surges through me.

"No, she isn't. I don't care what her father does. I will *not* give her up."

"This isn't your choice anymore brother. We are already on our way to your place. She *is* coming with us. This was just a curtesy call. Nothing more."

I drop the phone and throw the blankets off me.

"Verity, Verity wake up. Now. Hurry."

She sits up with a fright, her eyes wide and confused.

"What's going on? Is my father here?" she stammers in fear.

"No, sorry. I didn't mean to scare you. But my brothers are coming to take you from me. I imagine they are on the way to my penthouse in the city, so we have less than an hour before they get there - realize their mistake and then come here."

"An hour for what? What is going to happen when they get here?" She asks.

"We aren't staying to find out. We're leaving."

"To go *where*?"

"Please, just get up. Grab whatever you need. We don't have time to discuss this now."

I leave Verity in the bedroom as I bolt downstairs to pack the essentials. Weapons, Kevlar, and my emergency go-bag which contains a medical kit and survival gear. I hope I need none of these items, but I'd rather be prepared and have them than leave them behind.

I set the items at the front door and run back upstairs to shove a few pieces of clothing into a leather duffel bag.

Verity has thrown some clothes into a suitcase as well.

She looks dazed and panicked.

"Do you have any idea where we'll go?" She asks.

"Yes, we can talk about it in the car. Are you almost ready?"

"Yes." She sighs, "I just need to get dressed." She is already pulling on a pair of jeans.

"I'll pack the car. Meet me downstairs." I grab her luggage and carry it with mine.

Fifteen minutes later we are on the road.

I don't have a plan. I don't know where we are going. I didn't want to tell her that in the house because she already looked so stressed.

Right now she has her eyes glued to the side mirror, watching the road behind us.

I reach out and run my hand over her thigh. "I'm watching our back. You can relax."

"I *can't* relax. This is so crazy." She snaps. "Where are we going, Red?"

I clench my jaw. I still don't want to tell her I have no idea. But I can't lie to her. What is the point of being together if I can't be straight with her.

"Right now, the plan is to get as far away from the city as possible. Its better we don't know where we'll stop because if we don't know - no one else can work it out either."

I can feel her eyes on me while I focus on the road.

I steal a glance at her and she softens her expression.

"Ok." She says, after a little while.

"Ok?" I'm surprised. I expected her to be furious because of my lack of planning.

"Yes. Ok." She snaps.

Over the next hour she sits with her eyes on the road ahead. Tension fills the car.

I didn't expect her father to react swiftly. I can't believe he launched an attack on one of our warehouses. This really is all out war.

I need time to think.

I need to keep Verity safe until I figure it all out.

The back roads are dark, and keep me off the main highways I drive with no route in mind. Turning here and there and not following any logical pattern or direction.

Verity shifts in her seat and turns her body slightly towards me.

"What pushed your brothers to come after me? They were angry before - but what made them get to where they agreed that taking me from you by force was the better option?"

I take a deep breath before answering her.

"Your father attacked our business." My fingers are gripping the steer wheel, my knuckles turning white.

She takes in a sharp, shaky breath.

"He attacked your family?" She gasps. "Was anyone hurt?"

"Three people died. My employees."

Verity presses her lips together, fighting tears.

"It's my fault." She whispers, her voice weak and pained.

"No, absolutely *not*. This is your *father's* fault. You didn't hurt those people - he did. All you did was fall in love. There is nothing wrong with loving someone, Verity. Everyone deserves love."

She turns her face away from me, looking out the window again and falling into silence once more.

I see a dirt road to the left and turn down it. The landscape is barren on either side of us. Long expanses of open grass lands, dried and empty, scattered with an occasional lone tree.

Crows caw in the sky above us, doing lazy circles as they hunt for food.

The air is crisp and dry out here and the sun is hot against my skin.

I have the window wide open, letting the grass scented breeze clear my thoughts. In the wind Verity's hair whips around her face, free and wild. Just as she should be.

I hate seeing her like this. She withdraws and tucks herself away somewhere.

She closes up when she gets scared and she lashes out when she gets angry.

I need to figure out a way to reach her, to make her understand I won't let anything happen to her.

Fifteen miles up the road I pull into a run down truck stop. There is a small coffee shop attached to it. Thick white chunks of old paint peel from the walls and wide cracks pattern the crumbling bricks beneath it.

"Let's get some food. Then we can drive a little more and find a place to stop for the day." I pull her door open and she climbs out, refusing to take my hand.

Sighing, I walk beside her. When I push the sand blasted glass door open a small bells chimes noisy above us and the old man behind the counter near the entrance looks up at us as though we've fallen from the sky.

"Are you lost?" he asks, scrunching his sun aged face in confusion.

"Not lost, just out on an adventure." I smile.

"If you're looking for adventure, you ain't gonna find it out here. There's nothing out here but truck stops and old motels."

I chuckle. "I guess it depends on what kind of adventure someone is looking for then."

He laughs too. A dry crackling sound that reminds me of my grandfather. He was a chain smoker.

"And you pretty thing. You also on an adventure?" he looks at Verity. She takes a step closer to me.

"Oh, don't mind me. I'm harmless." He laughs. "Ask my wife. I can't even run after ya or nothing."

He comes out from behind the counter, pushing the wheels of his wheelchair.

"Honey bee, we got visitors." He shouts into the back.

"Coming." A singsong voice replies to him.

"My wife is the best cook I've ever met. That's why our marriage lasted as long as it has." He grins.

His wife, a plump woman wearing a square shaped floral dress, comes walking towards us. "Is he giving you trouble?" she asks Verity with a warm smile on her face.

"No, not at all." Verity grins.

"You folks lost?"

"I already asked em that."

"Well?" She shrugs.

"Not lost, just hungry." I glance at Verity. She nods.

"In that case you are in the right place." Her husband's smile is so wide, and I can see pride in his eyes. "What's on the menu today, honey bee?"

"I've got a fresh load of cranberry bread just came out the oven. Still hot. And blueberry muffins and if you want something more substantial, I have lamb pot roast."

"Wow. It all sounds amazing." Verity says. She barely ate last night so I imagine she's starving.

We place an order for a bowl of pot roast and two thick slices of cranberry bread with apricot and strawberry jam.

Sitting at the table near the back of the coffee shop Verity is staring through the dusty window out onto the landscape.

"I've never been to a place like this." She comments.

I reach out and take her hand.

"Are you ok?" I ask.

She bites her lip. "This isn't really an adventure. Not the kind I would choose to go on."

"I know, little vixen. It's not the type of adventure I want to take you on either. We just need to get away for a while until I can figure things out."

She sighs loudly.

"How long will that take? A day? A week? A month?"

"I don't know."

She nods. Looking out the window again.

The old woman comes towards us carrying a tray of food.

She places it on our table. The pot roast smells incredible and my stomach growls with excitement.

"That's real butter." She says, placing a bowl on the table next to the bread.

"Thank you." Verity smiles. "It looks amazing."

"There's more. Just shout and I'll come running."

We both find the food surprisingly good. Verity jokes a little, but I can sense how uptight she is.

She's right.

This isn't an adventure. Our entire relationship has gone from being an adventure, a wild unknown, to become a stress.

As dramatic as it sounds we are on the run for our lives.

Her father has proven he is crazy enough to go to war to get her back and now I have to decide how to retaliate in order to force him to back down.

What terrifies me is just how far I will go to keep her.

I meant it when I said I would burn the world down for her.

As long as she and I stand together in the ashes afterward, it will be worth it.

After our lunch I purchased a few things from the kiosk. Snacks, cola, and a few bottles of water. Verity chooses a magazine and adds it to the pile on the counter.

When we walk back to the car Verity takes my hand and relief washes through me.

When we reach the car, I open the door for her but stop her from climbing in, instead I turn her to face me.

"I'll always be at your side, little vixen. I need you to know that. To believe it. I will never leave you." I say, staring into her bright blue eyes.

She reaches her hand up and traces her fingers over my jaw.

"I believe you, my Viking. I want to be with you forever too."

"Then we can be." I lean down and kiss her, relieved that she isn't pushing me away.

The tension in the car dissipated as they hit the road again. She has her hand on my leg and my fingers and intertwined through hers.

As long as she doesn't give up on me everything will turn out ok.

In fact, I won't *let* her give up on me. So everything *will be ok*.

An hour from the truck stop we find a motel.

I book us a room and unload our luggage from the car.

"We can stay here for a night or two. If we don't like it, we can drive farther on. The old man said there were a lot of places to choose from along this road."

"It's clean." She says, looking around the room. "Do you think we'll be safe here though?"

"No one will think to look for us here."

CHAPTER NINETEEN
Verity

The motel is like a graveyard. Desolate and lifeless.

Apart from the guy at the front desk we haven't seen a single other person in two days. On the road in the distance there are some trucks passing and when the wind is blowing too hard, I can see their dust trails rising into the air. But nothing else happens out here.

I am restless and uneasy, and the tension escalates the longer we remain here. I have nothing to distract me from my own thoughts.

Red believes that this is the safest place for us to hide, and I can see why. Because no one exists out here. *Nothing* exists.

He's powered off his phone, and I left mine behind, so we can't be tracked - but we also can't receive updates on the situation back home. Red is uncertain about the safety of his family, and I'm unsure if my father is causing chaos.

I swing back and forth between being furious at Red for bringing us here and being furious at myself for not just going home when my father told me to. But all of that is inconsequential when I think about leaving him - and I know I could never.

It doesn't stop the emotional turmoil though.

And with nothing else to do out here but think - I am going a little crazy.

I pick up a rock and throw it into the field behind the motel. I was out for a walk, but I've walked this path too many times and now I'm just sitting here on an old wooden bench that looks like it shouldn't still be functional.

I trace my finger over the gritty, dry surface and wince when a small splinter spikes into my skin.

"Dammit." I mutter.

"There you are." His voice comes from behind me.

"Where else would I be?" I snap, annoyed. I push and rub my finger to force the splinter out.

"I've got good news." Rufino says, sitting down on the bench next to me.

He has my full attention in an instant.

"We can go home?" I ask, excited and perking up, forgetting about the splinter.

"No, but the motel owner told me he was going past that truck stop we visited, and I asked him to bring us an order of whatever was on the menu today. Maybe we'll get some more of that incredible pot roast."

"Pot roast? Are you serious right now?" I get up with a loud huff and move to storm off. Rufino grabs my arm and pulls me onto his lap.

"Hey, don't do that. Don't walk away from me. I'm just trying to make the most of this situation."

I sit on his lap, annoyed that I like the way he is holding me and as always - how patient he is with me. My first instinct is to run. To lash out. To fight. His first instinct is to hold me. How did I find someone so perfect for me? Someone how knows exactly how to handle me in every situation. He's like the yin to my yang. My perfect balance. Someone to keep my grounded but still let me be wild and spontaneous.

Perhaps a little too spontaneous if I look around at where it's gotten us.

I sigh and Rufino chuckles.

He runs his hand up and down my spine, sending shivers through me and making me lean into him.

He grins and says, "It's not so bad. If I had to be stuck in a place like this with anyone on earth I'd choose you."

I laugh. "You *are* stuck in a place like this you idiot."

He chuckles too.

After a moment of silence, just us sitting together and looking out over the nothingness, he leans close and whispers against my ear.

"It won't be like this forever, my love. We will have our lives back to normal soon. This is only temporary."

"I'm just worried about where it all ends." I shrug,

my head resting on his shoulder and the warmth of his hand against my side.

"It ends with us together. No matter what." He says.

He wraps his hand around the back of my neck and digs his fingers into my skin. His expression becomes serious.

"I am never letting you go, Verity. You and I belong together. Nothing in this universe can change that. If I can't be with you I don't want to exist."

My heart races at his words.

His love for me is an obsession.

It makes me feel desired and dangerously romantic.

I turn on his lap so that I'm facing him. Wrapping my legs around his waist I lean forward to kiss him.

He grabs my ass and pushes his cock up against me. It's hard and pressing against the fabric of his pants, teasing me.

A soft moan escapes my lips and I kiss deeper, pushing my tongue into his mouth.

Never in my life have I been so loved before. No one has ever wanted me before. So needed.

His love for me drives me crazy in passionate ways. Pushes me to do things that even *I* might not do alone. He is the one person in this world who might be a little crazier than I am.

He stands up, lifting me in his arms.

"I think we should go somewhere a little more private." He grins.

"More private than the middle of nowhere?"

"I'm sure old man Tucker at reception would love to come back early and get an eye full of your gorgeous ass. I'd bet he's never seen something so beautiful in his entire life." He says slapping my butt to prove his point.

I giggle and press my mouth over his to kiss him while he carries me towards our motel room. He kicks the bottom of the door open with his foot and then closed again behind us before he drops me onto the bed.

Red pulling his shirt off, so I do the same. I tug my t-shirt over my head and throw it at him with a mischievous smile on my face.

He stands next to the bed looking down at me with intense focus.

"You try are the most beautiful thing in the world, Verity. I could obsess over you for all eternity. You are my reason to live - my everything."

My heart beats faster, pushing the boundaries of my love for him further than ever before. His pale green eyes are my drug, and his words are a poison of dangerous proportions. I want him.

Standing up on the bed I jump over to him and into his arms, wrapping my arms around his neck and my legs around his waist.

"I love you to the end of the universe, Viking." I kiss his cheek, then nuzzle my face into his neck. "And then all the way back again. A hundred times."

He falls us both onto the bed, his arms pinned on either side of my head, pressing his hands into the mattress, caging me into his field of vision.

"Believe me when I tell you I will never leave you or stop loving you." He whispers, looking down at me with a hungry fierceness in his eyes.

I reach up to touch his face.

"Why me? How did I get so lucky?"

"It was always going to be you, Verity. It wasn't luck. It was destiny."

Outside the motel room a loud screech of tires skidding across gravels makes us both freeze. The door flies open, slamming against the old brick wall behind it and causing it to splinter.

Three men rush into the room dressed head to toe in black - then two more. I scream as fear floods through my body.

Heavily armed guards pack the small motel room, pointing their weapons at us.

Rufino moves, spinning to face them and shoving me protectively behind his body.

He holds me there with one arm behind his back.

"Who the fuck are you?" he snarls, facing down the men without a hint of fear in his voice.

My heart beats, almost drowning out sound.

Wrapping my arm around my breasts to cover them but also for a false sense of security.

Outside someone chuckles.

"It's my father's men." I gasp in shock, recognizing that cold steel mocking laugh.

"How?" Rufino demands.

"Get up." One man demands, waving the barrel of his rifle at Rufino.

He stands up slowly, pulling me with him so that I am still behind him.

Rufino squats down at grabs my t-shirt off the floor, passing it behind himself to me.

"Put it on, my love." He mutters.

"That's right. It's time to get dressed and end this disgusting interaction." My father's voice comes from outside the door.

"How?" I whisper again, trying to figure out if there was any way he could have tracked me - but I have nothing on me. It doesn't make sense.

My father steps into the room and tilts his head to the side, eyeing Rufino.

"Did you really think you could win against me?" he asks, calm and deadly. Then he turns to me. "Verity, make yourself decent. Put your shoes on for fuck sakes, we're leaving."

"You're not taking her anywhere. You'll have to kill me first."

"I have no problem with that." My father laughs again.

"No." I scream, stepping out from behind him. "Please, don't."

"Then do as you're told." His eyes are empty. Like dark pits filled with nothing but coal. Dead.

I reach out and touch Rufino's side. My fingers trace over his skin. "Red. Don't." I beg him. But his body is tense. His stance tells me he is no intention of letting me go without a fight.

Several guns pointed towards him tells me he doesn't stand a chance.

"Red." I plead again.

"I made you a promise." He says, his voice low.

"It's not worth your life."

"Enough." My father snarls, "Take her. Let's go."

One of his men grabs my arm and yanks me away from Rufino. I scream with fright as the man's rough fingers dig into my skin.

Rufino turns into a beast at the sound of my pain.

He flies at the man closest to him, slamming his fist into the guys face. I hear the crack of bone as his nose splinters under the force of Rufino's punch.

Rufino doesn't stop. From the floor he grabs another man's leg and yanks it out from beneath him. He falls hard onto his back, causing his gun to fire.

My father ducks to the ground yelling something I can't make out.

Three other men fly towards Rufino. One of them kicks him in the face and his head snaps backwards, but it doesn't stop him. He's back on his feet as their hands grab at him and try to force him back down.

"Rufino, stop." I scream. "He'll kill you."

Tears are streaming down my cheeks.

My entire body is shaking, and my voice is breaking.

"Stop." I scream again.

Someone lifts the butt of his rifle and slams it into Rufino's head.

He collapses to the ground, semi-unconscious, groaning and lifting his hand to touch his skull at the point of impact.

I try to run to him, but hands grab at me and pull me away.

I stand with my eyes on him, my back against the guard, his hand around my throat and a gun against my head.

Inside my body is raging. I want to go to Rufino. I want to know he's ok.

CHAPTER TWENTY
Rufino

The world is spinning in and out of darkness while I fight against it. She needs me. She needs me now more than ever. I can't let them take her.

I promised to keep her safe.

I push myself up onto my arms. Squeezing my eyes shut for a second to force away the fog infecting my head.

Pain shoots down my neck and into my shoulder. My skull is about to explode with pain.

It doesn't matter.

All that matters is her.

I push myself up onto my haunches and then stand on shaky legs.

Her voice is swimming in and out of my mind.

"Rufino - are you ok - Rufino?" There's a quiver of tears in her words.

They fuel me, driving me and giving me the strength I need to stand.

When I spin around, I throw another punch at the guy standing closest to me.

He falls to the floor.

"Enough." Luca screams.

Two men lift their rifles to my head, the barrels pushed against my skull. I freeze and look towards Verity, trapped against another man, his gun against her temple. "No." I mutter, hopeless to save her.

Luca pushes one man out of his way and stands glaring at me. He's close enough that I can smell the stale heat of his breath.

"I would have killed you if it were up to me." He snarls.

"You are going to regret not killing me." I assure him. "When I come after you and tear your world apart, brick by brick. It's not too late to walk away now and leave us in peace."

He laughs.

"Are you fucking stupid? Look how easy it was to get to you. Your own family gave you up."

"What?" I stammer.

"How the fuck do you think I found you?" he laughs.

"My brothers—"

"You didn't know your car had tracking installed on it, did you? A second device linked to their security systems, not yours."

I shake my head. No, this can't be happening.

"Masaccio was more than happy to give me the location, but he made me promise to leave you alive. And - I am a man of my word. But you are testing my patience, Rufino Vece, and if I have to go back to your brother and tell him there was an accident and one gun went off - well—"

"Dad." Verity sobs. "I'll come with you. I won't fight. Please leave him alone."

Luca spins towards his daughter. "You are disgusting, Verity. I am ashamed of you. Ashamed to call you my own." He hisses into her face. She winces away from him and the man holding her prisoner tightens his grip around her throat.

My insides are like liquid. Lava, thick and hot, burning away everything inside me. The pain of betrayal, confusing my family being willing to throw me to the wolves like this - *the anger.*

"Let's go." Luca demands and one at a time I watch his men leave, and I watch Verity being dragged away from me.

She doesn't fight.

She gets into the back of the car without even trying to push them away.

I know she has to. I know she has no choice.

But what cuts me deep in my heart is that she doesn't even look back - not once.

Listening to the sound of their engines starting and the tires crunching against old dry gravel as one by one they drive away from the motel - it's pure torture. I stand frozen for a long time, aching in every inch of my body, my heart shattered and my soul sinking fast.

I don't know how long I am lost in my anger for, but when I snap out of it the sun is gone. The night sky is dark, pierced with sharp points of light where millions of stars shine like bullets in the blackness.

I look down at my fists, bleeding, the skin torn off my knuckles. Then I look around the motel room.

I trashed it.

I don't remember doing it.

The bed rests on its side against the wall, and the lamps are shattered. The small wooden table and chair from the corner are lying in broken pieces near the bathroom door. The windows are glittering shards of glass, patterned across the old worn carpet.

My breath is heavy. My chest is tight.

I blacked out and let my rage loose on this room.

Clenching my fists I let out a gut wrenching scream.

There is no time for this. I should chase after her already.

I grab my things, toss them into the backseat of my car and floor the gas back towards the city.

"I'm coming for you, little vixen." My voice is a low growl in the chilly night air.

I drive with a single focus.

To find her.

But where do I start? And how can I do this alone? Because my brothers have clarified that they have no intention of helping me. In fact, they would rather help her father - our enemy - instead of helping their own brother.

This marks another moment of truth. Their wordless confession of their disloyalty to me. Their belief that I don't belong with them.

Fuck them all.

Every single one of them can burn in hell for all I care.

Verity is my universe, my everything.

Tears fall from my eyes, rolling silent and deadly down my cheeks. I brush them away with anger in my heart. I've never cried in my life. But I've also never lost something this important to me.

I drive without stopping until I reach my penthouse in the city. I need to get online and start trying to figure out where Luca would have taken his daughter for safe keeping. He's not a stupid man. Yes, his conceit is impossible to ignore. Cold and cruel, yes. But not stupid. Knowing I'm coming for him, he will be prepared.

The penthouse is empty, dark and uninviting. I am so used to having Verity by my side, close, in the next room. Even when we are fighting, I still had the comfort of her being near to me. Maybe I should have gone to my mansion where I might still smell her on the bedsheets. There would be remnants of her lying around. A hint. A warmth in the air.

There is nothing here.

With a pounding headache pulsing from the back of my skull I sit down at my computer and open the security app.

My phone rings.

Masaccio.

I pull the green button across the screen I set the phone to speaker and leave it lying on the desk.

"Rufino, my brother, I see you've just got back to the city." He says.

My jaw clenches the pain of it vies with the pain of the headache.

"Rufino - we had to do it." He tries to reason with me.

"Fuck you, Masaccio." I snarl.

"You need to understand. You were asking us to risk everyone over one girl."

"Not just any girl. *My* girl. *My wife.*"

"Be reasonable, Red. Come on, man. This is ludicrous. The safety of your own family —"

"I have no family. I only have her."

"For fuck's sake." He mutters. "You're a fucking idiot. We did what was best for everyone - including you. You were on the run. You can't live like that."

"This conversation is over, Masaccio. Don't call me again."

"What are you going to do?" he shouts, trying to continue the conversation before I hang up.

"Whatever it takes. Whatever I have to do to get her back."

"Leave it alone—"

I click the red button to end the call and stare at the phone for a moment.

Whatever it takes.

I only realize I haven't eaten or slept when I get dizzy with exhaustion and hunger.

It's been almost thirty-six hours since I last saw Verity. Thirty-six hours and I've found nothing that might lead me to her.

But I'm no good to anyone in this state. I must sleep so that I can clear my head and start again in a few hours.

I push away from my desk and in a fit of rage I almost smash my laptop.

"Where the fuck is she?" I scream and it echoes through the penthouse.

Staggering, I walk to my bedroom and collapse onto the bed.

Dark visions haunt my dreams, intensifying my anger.

Masaccio is standing over Verity, smirking. The gun in his hand catches the light when he lifts it and points it at her head. She's on the floor, her legs folded to the side. She lifts her hands up over her face and cries out in fear.

I try to run towards her, but my feet at sinking in thick black liquid. An oily, unforgiving syrup that is creeping up my legs. "Verity." I scream.

They are moving further away from me. Masaccio turns to look at me and his eyes are empty sockets. Black holes of nothingness.

"For the family." He says, his voice robotic and his movements stiff.

His finger squeezes against the trigger and a sharp snap pulses through the air when the bullet fires from the gun.

Time moves slower. I can see the air moving, leaving a

spinning trail behind the tail of the bullet as it arches towards her skull.

"Verity." I scream again but now I'm underwater.

When I open my mouth, the liquid pours into my lungs and I can't breathe.

I'm drowning. Kicking against nothing. The surface is so far above me I will never make it in time.

I reach up, towards the piercing rays of light stabbing into the dark blue endlessness around me.

Shadows swim beneath me.

I can't see her anywhere.

I can't escape.

"Verity." Her name falls from my lips and I find myself in my bed, sitting upright, sweat pooling off me.

My legs tangle in the blankets, and my pillow is soaked through with perspiration and dried blood.

I rub my eyes I try to push the nightmare away.

Masaccio's empty eyes are clear in my mind.

Kicking the blankets away I look at the time. Three hours. I slept for three hours. It's too long.

Anything could have happened to her during that time and I wasted it.

Shower. Eat. I have to keep moving.

The ice cold water hits my skin and makes every muscle in my body tense up. It pulls me awake though. That's all I need.

Blood washes away from the wound on my skull, running in dark red streams over my naked skin, down onto the stark white tiles of the shower floor. It swirls and pools and then slips away, down the drain.

I stand under the cold flow until the water runs clear and my thoughts are less chaotic.

With a towel wrapped around my waist I rummage through the kitchen cupboards looking for something to eat. Frozen meals in the freezer, a packet of chips in the cupboard.

I toss a lasagna into the microwave and turn it on while I go upstairs to get dressed.

I need to pull a list of every property her father owns. If I had access to my computers at work, it would be easy. But my brothers would have locked me out. I'll have to get in contact with the hacker.

It's amazing what you can do when you throw money at a problem.

Dressed, fed and almost human again, I climb into my car and head into town. This is not something I want to do over the phone. I don't trust anyone. I'll give him the job face to face.

CHAPTER TWENTY-ONE
Verity

"I hate you." I whisper towards the man in front of me.

My father turns in his seat and scowls at me. "Hate? After everything I've done for you?" he snaps angrily. "You ungrateful little bitch. I saved you from *yourself*. You are a danger, a loose cannon. I can't trust you to behave in any kind of decent manner."

I shake my head, sitting in the backseat of his car with security guards on either side of me. My father is in the front seat. He huffs before looking forward again, but I can see his eyes on me in the rearview mirror.

"I'm ashamed of you." He snarls.

"Ha." I laugh. "How can you be ashamed of the person you created? I am the way I am because you *made* me this way." I hiss.

I see his fists clench in his lap. "If you were how I made you, you'd be obedient and placid."

I stare past the security guard at my side, ignoring the rifle on his lap. I look out of the window at the scenery whipping past the car. We've been driving for hours. I'm tired. I'm scared. I'm worried about Rufino and all I want is to be back in his arms.

Obedient. I chuckle. If my father thought that overbearing control was going to create an obedient daughter he was mistaken.

"All of your rules, all of your attempts to stop me from living my life - they made me this defiant. I had no choice but to fight back against you so that I could find out who *I* was."

"Who you are doesn't matter." He shouts. I see the guard next to me tense up. "You are nothing but what I say you are." My father blurts out.

This conversation is getting me nowhere. It's stealing my energy. Energy I need to save for when Rufino comes to rescue me.

My father has a deeply ingrained inability to understand anyone's opinion or perspective other than his own.

I've tried so many times to reason with him throughout my life. To make him see things from my point of view. It's *never* worked. Not even once. I can't imagine that changing now.

"What are you going to do with me?" I sigh, thinking of the convent in Europe. I'm delighted to be going that way since it would be simple to get away from there. They won't be prepared for someone like me. I'm smarter than their systems and useless little locks. I'll get out, I'll contact Rufino and he can come and fetch me. We'll run away again. This time we won't be found, and we'll never come back.

We can be together.

I close my eyes and lean my head against the backrest of the car.

My father hasn't answered my question. He isn't going to. He likes to keep his plans muted because it's another form of control for him.

I'm too tired to push him. I've been pushing him since we drove away from the motel. I was so heartbroken I couldn't turn my head to look back at Rufino. I couldn't process the idea of leaving him behind.

Now I regret it.

But when I close my eyes, I can see his face. I can feel his touch against my skin. If I keep my eyes closed, I can pretend I'm with him.

I must have dozed off in the car because I wake up to a guard shoving me. "We're here. Get out." He snaps.

"Where?" I stammer, confused and annoyed.

"Get the fuck out. Stop wasting my time." He points his gun at me.

I look forward, but the rest of the car is empty.

My father isn't in the front seat anymore. The car is parked underground somewhere. I recognize nothing.

Sliding across the leather seats I climb out of the car and stand next to the angry security guard. I don't recognize him either. Another new recruit.

None of the men last long with my father. This one won't either.

He'll fire him, or the guy will just disappear, of his own accord or my fathers. Anyone who disagrees with my father disappears.

"Move." He huffs, jabbing the barrel of his rifle into my ribs.

"What the fuck is your problem? Calm down, asshole." I snap back at him.

He pushes me towards a grey door. I open it and step through.

It leads into a dingy foyer with an elevator in the corner. The place smells of dust. Stuff and cold.

"The elevator." He commands.

I push the button a few times in annoyance. Then stand back and wait for it to arrive.

The silence is awkward and tense. Where is my father? What is this place?

A soft chime beeps through the air and the metal doors slide open.

I step inside before he tells me to because I don't want to be jabbed with a rifle again. My ribs are already bruised, when I poke them they are spongy and breathing is painful.

He knocks the butt of his gun against the number seventeen and the doors slide closed.

His breathing is so loud. It's annoying.

Everything is annoying.

We ride slowly to the seventeen floor and the asshole pushes me out of the elevator into a hallway. "Move, dammit." He snarls.

I lift my hands in a sign of surrender, hoping to ease his aggressiveness. All the while I'm taking everything in, counting how many paces from the elevator. I look to see an escape route.

A door at the end of the hallway is open. I walk towards it, assuming that's our destination.

I don't know what I expected to see when I walked through the doorway, but a nice, clean apartment was not it.

Its modern and bright with enormous windows

spread across two walls of the corner apartment that let a lot of natural light in.

"What is this place? Who lives here?" I ask, stepping inside.

My father's voice answers me, coming from the kitchen on the right.

"This is the safe house where you will be staying."

My mouth drops open. How will Rufino find me here?

"Please, let me go home rather."

"You don't belong at home. I don't want that kind of trouble in my house because you can't be trusted.

"I'm your daughter, not some prisoner." I shout.

A sharp slap stings across my face.

I turn to face the guard who dared to hit me. I'm waiting for my father to tell him he's fired. To kick him out. To tell him he's done for daring to touch me.

"Don't speak to your father like that." He says, his eyes tracing over my body.

I look him up and down, furious at the audacity of this man.

"Who the hell do you think—"

"Thank you, Roger." My father says, grateful because this random asshole just slapped me through the face.

I spin towards my father with an expression of shock on my face.

"If you don't care what happens to me, then just *let me go.*" I demand.

He shakes his head. "You're wrong sweetheart. I care. I care about how your behavior affects the family name. I care about what people think when they look at you and know that you carry my blood in your veins."

I am finally beginning to understand.

My father never cared about me as his daughter. Only for what I represented in the public eye. It's the reason he never accepted me.

It's the reason he fought me on everything. I am supposed to be a replica of him. A mirror image of his choices and his life.

He will never let me free.

He will never allow me to live my life the way I want to.

Desperation seeps into my pores. I am an animal in a cage, and he is the ring master. Poking me with a stick and demanding I do the tricks he wants to see.

Genuine panic floods me. I can't stay here. I will never see the light of day again.

Without thinking it through I run.

There is no proper plan to get out of here, but I have to try.

I bolt straight for the open door I dodge the outreached hand of the guard standing closest to me.

Someone behind me cocks their gun.

"Don't fucking shoot her your idiot." My father snaps. "Bring her back."

I hear nothing else because I am half way to the elevator already.

I've never run this fast in my life.

My lungs are burning when I reach the silver doors.

Gratitude overwhelms me when I see the elevator is waiting there. I skid into it and slam my hand repeatedly against the G button.

"Close dammit. Please close." I yell at the doors.

They're getting closer. Their heavy black boots are loud down the enclosed hallway.

The doors close.

I hold my breath.

Just as the doors slide the last few inches closed their angry faces appear in the gap. But they were too slow. And now I'm free.

I grin as the elevator carries me down to the parking garage again.

Not knowing where I am in the city is going to make this more challenging, but it's ok. I'll find a way. As long as I am out of my father's reach there is a chance.

However, when the doors slide open again I am staring at the barrel of a gun.

My heart sinks.

I was stupid to think he didn't have additional guards on the ground. My father is known for his cautious nature and placing extra men at every corner.

The guy steps into the elevator with a smirk, forcing me to take a step backwards as the gun presses into my forehead.

"Hi, sweetheart. Were you going somewhere?" he laughs.

I bite my lip. Tense. Hopeless. Terrified that I will never see Rufino again.

I don't want to exist in a world where we are not together.

The guard shoves me back into the small apartment.

My father is sitting cross-legged on the sofa, waiting for my return.

"Verity, you have used up my last thread of patience." He says, standing up.

"Dad, please let me go. Please don't do this." I beg.

"Lock her in the room and stand guard outside the door. The man who lets her escape will get a bullet in his skull. Is anything about what I've said unclear?"

"No, sir." They chorus in response.

Rough hands push me into the room and the room door slams shut behind me. I hear the lock clicking into place.

It's a beautiful room, with crispy white bedding and a neat adjoining bathroom. Under different circumstances I wouldn't mind being stuck in here for a while. But this is a prison. I don't see the modern decor or soft lighting, all I see are four walls keeping me away from the man that I love.

A holding cell designed for nothing other than my heartache.

I curl up on the bed, crying from the overwhelming helpless feelings that are drowning me.

I want to have hope - but I'm also scared of it.

Because now I will find out if Red really meant everything he said to me.

Will he tear the world apart for me? Will he burn it to the ground to find me?

Or was it all just a game to him?

Something to fill the time in between the monotony of general life.

For me it was real.

I've never felt love like that before.

I can only wait now - to find out if he is coming to save me.

CHAPTER TWENTY-TWO
Rufino

Collision has a full house tonight.

Everything here reminds me of her and it's making me sick to my stomach.

I need her.

I yearn for her, it's crushing me inside. I came here to find one of Verity's friends. To see if I could get any information about where she might be. But none of them have seen her since before we got married. They haven't spoke to her.

She's disappeared off the map.

Music vibrates through my body as I scan the sea of faces, dancing, laughing, celebrating life as though they have something to live for.

I've been searching and finding nothing but dead ends and bad leads for days now. Without Verity, I'm losing my mind. I can sense it slipping away from me. She is my stability. She keeps me grounded.

The barmen sets another shot of vodka in front of me. I pick it up and toss it back, letting it burn down my throat. The alcohol is numbing the pain for a moment. I'm so drained, so exhausted, that I don't know what to do.

I slam the empty shot glass down on the counter top.

"Another." I demand, then change my mind. "Just leave the fucking bottle." I can see the judgement in his eyes, but I don't give a fuck. They know who I am, and they know better than to deny me what I want.

He sets it down in front of me and backs away with a sour look on his face.

Fuck him.

Fuck everyone.

Picking up the bottle I drink straight from it.

Taking long gulps of the crystal clear poison. I want to feel less.

This is my only option. In no time at all the blurry vision and slurred thoughts are making me laugh. It's not amusement. It's not happiness. It's pure anger.

Anger because the world took away the *one* beautiful thing I had in my life.

Anger because nothing has meaning without her.

Anger because I'm failing.

I made her a promise. I was supposed to keep her safe. I was supposed to keep her with me.

I have failed her, and I don't know how to fix it.

I step away from the bar, shove a guy out of my way as I stumble forward. He was dancing too close. Annoying me.

He trips and hits leg on a table.

"You fucker." He shouts, turning to face me.

Oh, *yes*, I want this. I want to fight him. I laugh louder.

He raises his hands in the air, appearing much calmer. "Wait, bro, it's ok. It was my fault. I'm sorry. No problem, man. I'm sorry." He steps back so fast he trips again, then scoots away across the floor.

"Weak." I scream at him and several people in the club turn to glare at me but just as quickly they turn away again.

In a blind fit I smash the bottle across the same table he tripped over. Glass shatters around me.

"Does nobody want to fight me?" I shout. "Are you all scared? Is life too precious?"

Around me a wide space opens up as people scamper to create distance from me.

I spin in a slow circle with my arms spread wide. I need this.

"There must be *someone*?"

"He's over there. Please, get him out of here." I turn towards the voice and see one of their bouncers - standing next to Masaccio and Tuomo.

"Fuck." I growl.

Mas storms over to me and tries to grab the broken bottle from my hand. I move to the side and duck away from him.

"Rufino you have to leave before the cops get here. They've already been called. They gave us a head start as a courtesy to the family, but they are on the way."

"Let them come." I laugh. "Let them try and take me."

"You've lost your mind." Tuomo says, trying to grab my arm.

I'm seeing two of both of them which is amusing because they're already identical twins and now there are four of them swaying back and forth in front of my vision. I point at their blurred faces and mock them with my anger.

"Grab him, we have to drag him out. We can't be attracting this much attention." Mas mutters to Tuomo.

He steps close to me and I swing my fist.

He wasn't expecting it and with one shot I send him flying backwards.

"You mother fucker." Tuomo hisses and comes running at me. His shoulder slams into my chest and all the air of knocked from my lungs. I gasp, fighting confusion for a moment, then I start beating my elbow into the back of his head until he lets me go.

He flies at me again, angry and over my shit by the looks of things.

But I'm not backing down. I hate them.

I hate them for what they did.

I hate them more than I hate her father because I expected more from my family.

A mistake I will never make again.

The fight grows steadily more violent.

Masaccio tries to step in between us, and I fling the broken bottle at his face. It cuts him across the cheek before it splinters into pieces behind him.

My hand is bleeding, but I don't know what from. When I grab Tuomo around the throat, the blood dripping between my fingers makes it slippery and sticky.

Tuomo is on his back, lying on the floor beneath me. I now have both of my hands wrapped around his throat, and his eyes are bulging from his head.

His lips are turning blue. The panic in his eyes is more than satisfying. It's perfect.

I squeeze tighter.

Masaccio leaps onto my back, clawing at my throat, locking his elbow around my neck and trying to pull me away from our brother.

"You'll kill him. *Stop, Rufino.*" Masaccio screams against my ear.

"I'll kill both of you." I scream back, my eyes narrowing with determination. My arm muscles ripple as I try to break Tuomo's neck with the weight of my body.

Masaccio presses something against the side of my throat and a million volts of lightening snap through me like sharp blades of ice. My body convulses and spasm - completely out of my control. I fall to the side.

Tuomo is no longer beneath me. I am leaning against the floor fighting for air while every muscle in my body screams at me.

The pain of being tasered is dark.

A grin spreads across my face and I wipe the spit away from my lips.

"Again." I turn towards Masaccio. "Do it again"

This time the taser knocks me out.

All I see is the floor coming up towards my face at incredible speed. Then nothing. Blissful peace. The first moment of peace I've had since I lost her.

No dreams. No haunting nightmares.

Next I know I'm outside the club - music pulsing behind me from behind the walls. Its muffled. Only the steady beat of bass reaching the open night air.

I'm being held up between the twins, their arms wrapped beneath mine, supporting me as they drag me towards the car.

Fuck this. I'm not going with them.

I kick my feet into the ground and throw myself backwards. I'm too big for them to hold. Tuomo swears.

"Fucking asshole." He snarls.

"Get in the fucking car." Masaccio demands, pointing at the car as though I was a kid, and he was the parent, dictating and controlling.

"Go fuck yourselves." I snarl, then turn and run.

I'm too drunk to see which direction I'm headed in and I don't care. I just need to escape those fucking back stabbing mother fuckers who took the only thing in the world that I want and *gave her away*.

That they think I'll let that go - forgive them - be ok with them - they are the crazy ones.

Images flash through my mind of Tuomo with protruding eyes and blue lips. I flex my fists as I run.

I was going to kill him.

I wanted to.

I would have.

And even now - I don't trust myself not to kill them if I get into that car with them. They are safer if they just let me go.

I'm not looking for revenge against them - not yet, anyway.

All I'm trying to do is get back to her.

If I can't - if I cannot find her - then they will reap the wrath of that pain.

For now I still have hope. Dwindling and feint, but I'm not giving up.

I won't ever give up.

I run until my lungs scream and a stitch tightens my ribs. I run because it burns. It hurts everywhere. The pain is a pleasure I need. It'll keep me sharp and burn the alcohol away.

When I stop, gasping for air, folded double with my hand pressed against my ribs, I'm at the docks. A rich scent of salt and boat fuel drift around this place giving it a distinct smell. Mixed with the smell of seals and raw fish.

I stand up, flexing my shoulders and rolling my neck.

My feet thud on the wooden jetty floating between massive yachts as I walk towards the end.

Its pitch dark and deadly silent. The only sound is the ocean water, lapping against the sides of those boats. Pristine, glossed white and blue. I'd like to take Verity on one of theses. Sail her around the world, we could escape everyone. Watch sunsets. Be alone.

I sit with a loud huff on a chunky wooden pole. A thick rope is wrapped around it. My eyes follow the rope up towards the boat that is anchored to the dock here.

Burn it all down. A voice in my head encourages me.

Burn it to the ground. Burn everything. Until you find her.

I pull a silver lighter out of my back pocket. The metal body engraved with a snake. Flicking it back and forth in my fingers I spark a flame and then snap the lid closed over it to smother it out again.

Burn it.

Burn everything.

The thought won't let go.

It's the answer. The solution to finding her.

Standing with renewed enthusiasm I pick up a small barrel of fuel sitting near the loading area of the yacht. The menacing grin on my face would send chills through anyone who looked my way. But there is no one here. Not a soul around.

Tossing the bottle cap into the water I throw the open fuel can into the deck of the closest yacht. Then I spark my lighter to life. For a moment I watch the flame dance in the quiet night air.

With a quick flick of my wrist I throw the lighter onto the yacht as well.

For a second nothing happens.

Then a wall of fire explodes up from the deck of the boat.

It throws me off balance and I land hard on my ass on the jetty. Laughing like a mad man.

"Burn it all down. Burn everything until you find her." I scream against the heat pushing towards me.

Standing up I dust my hands over my pants.

It's time to go. I have things to do.

I have a plan. *Finally*, I have a plan.

I'm going to see if my hacker friend has come up with a list of Luca A'Vara's properties.

I will burn them down - one by one - until he gives her back to me.

As promised, I will take everything from him. He will beg me to stop but I won't. I will keep going until she is in my arms.

CHAPTER TWENTY-THREE
Verity

I haven't slept for days.

Not since I got here. But I lost count. I don't know how longs it's been.

Everything is blurring together in one long stream of nothingness.

Sometimes I sit and gaze at the white curtains, other times I curl up on the bed and cry.

Right now, I am pressing my knees up against my chin and squeezing my eyes closed.

I can still see his face in my mind.

His beautiful dark red beard, the angular shape of his jaw. Those piercing, pale green eyes.

Where is he?

I have never needed someone as much in my life.

But not just anyone. It has to be him. I need him.

No one has come into this room to speak to me since they slammed the door closed. I'm alone it's making me go crazy.

The only sign that I'm *not* alone in this apartment is the hand that slides food through the slot in the locked door twice a day.

They don't speak to me. They don't answer me when I push the slot open from my side and scream into it.

They haven't acknowledged my existence and I'm wondering if I might have died - and this is hell.

Tailor made to break me down.

I've been thinking about my life and how I spent my time. The friends I selected, and why.

Sammy, Bella, and Dante seem like people I knew in some different time line. Or another life perhaps.

My life before Rufino.

The parties, surrounded by so many people who never met the true me - they are just shallow memories compared to the brief time I've spent with Rufino.

My friends weren't real friends. They were there for the VIP tables and endless bottles of alcohol. They were quick to say yes to a night out - but I've never had a genuine conversation with any of them. And when I get bored with the crowd I've hung out with for a while I replace them. Was I the problem?

Why be angry about the choices that led me to discovering Red? My destiny.

I never connected with my father and I never connected with my friends.

The only person I've ever had anything real with - is Rufino.

I roll onto my back and stare at the ceiling. It's the only part of this apartment that has any character. Pale water stains have seeped through the paint in pretty patterns edged with dark lines.

It's the only imperfection in here.

I stare at it for long enough that it puts me in a trance.

Images of my mother flash through my mind. I never got to meet her, not when I was old enough to remember it, and I only know her through photographs. The very few that my father has shown me.

She was beautiful.

I see myself in her and I can't count the number of times I've wished I could have met her. I also can't count the amount of times my father snarled at me - telling me I was just like her as though it was an insult. He doesn't know that the more he told me that the more I became *me* - or her. Everything that annoyed him becoming more stressed and defined.

He told me she left because of me. Because she wanted to escape me.

I've always known it wasn't true. In my heart I knew she would never have done that.

Our housekeeper told me the truth when I was about six, confirming what I already believed.

My mother loved me deeply. She had nothing but warmth for me. She would sit for hours, singing while she rocked me on her lap. Her eyes would light up when I laughed. She loved me. No one can take that from me.

But one day, before my first birthday, she disappeared. And my father threatened everyone in the house that if they spoke of her again, he would cut their tongues out.

The day after the housekeeper told me the truth she disappeared too.

If I stare at the water stain long enough, it looks like a serpent, curling over the ceiling, trying to crush the apartment with its long muscular body. I am lying in the snake's belly. Trapped and desperate for air.

The door lock clicks, and I bolt upright on the bed.

My eyes tuned onto the moving handle.

I'm holding my breath. Terrified and excited at the same time. I want to see another human being - but I *want* it to be Rufino.

The door swings open and my father steps into the room.

I let out a heavy sigh.

He pulls his mouth tight.

"You look like shit. Have you showered since you got here?" he snaps, tossing a set of fresh clothes onto the bed. I stare at them, then I stare at him, not saying a word.

He paces around the room as though he was strolling through a park on a summers day. His hands tucked into his pockets.

When he gets to the window, he reaches up and yanks the curtain open, flooding the space with glaring white light.

I blink against it, scrunching my eyes to narrow slits.

"Where is Rufino?" I mutter, finally finding my voice.

"Speak up, girl, I can't understand you." He huffs, looking bored.

"Where is Rufino?" I scream, my fingers digging into the blankets.

My father laughs, tilting his head to the side while he watches me with amusement.

"He's not coming. Haven't you figured it out by now? You were nothing but a game for him. A little side fling. *Entertainment*. He used you, Verity and you fell for it hook, line, and sinker."

"You're wrong about him."

"I'm not. The only report I've had about the man you love, since you last saw him, is that he was seen at Collision, partying up a storm. Enjoying his life and freedom from the burden of you. He's already forgotten about you. You are nothing but a blip in his past now."

I shake my head. It can't be true. He's just saying that to mess with me.

Swallowing hard to push the tears away because I don't want my father to see me crying, I stand up off the bed. I'm lightheaded from not eating enough and my clothes smell of sweat.

I did shower, but I had nothing else to change into.

My father looks me up and down and his lips curl into an expression of disgust.

"Shower. Then come out and have dinner with me in the living room." He sighs.

"Are you going to let me go?" I ask, glaring at him with defiance.

"No, Verity. Until you accept that your life belongs to me, you will never leave this room."

"How do you decide that?" I scream. "What makes your choices better than mine?"

He walks up to me and grabs my face in his hands.

"You look just like her." His fingers dig into my cheeks, then he pushes my head to the side and lets go, wiping his hand off on his pants as though I was something dirty.

"You killed her didn't you." I whisper, filled with hate.

The edges of his mouth curl up into a grotesque smile.

"I don't know why you would think that." He shrugs, acting innocent.

"Now clean up, get dressed, and come have dinner with me."

"No." I say again, glaring at him. "Just kill me now and get it over with."

He slaps me hard across the face. Heat and pain burn into my cheek.

"Then rot in here until you die." He snarls, spinning away from me and storming towards the door.

It slams shut behind him.

The locks clicks into place.

And I am alone again.

I'd rather be alone and going crazy than spend time with my father.

As much as I have never known love until I met Rufino - I also never understood hate until I looked at my father right now.

The coldness in his eyes can't hide who he really is anymore. I see straight through him.

I used to fear him. I might even have respected him at one point..

But now I see him for what he is. A heartless monster who takes what he wants and doesn't give a shit about anyone else but himself.

I wouldn't blame my mother for leaving.

But if she had she would've taken me with her.

She's dead.

And he's the one who killed her.

And when Rufino finds me - he will kill my father.

Picking up the fresh clothes from the end of the bed I carry them through to the bathroom. I flick the shower on and stare at it for a moment.

My thoughts are fragments and scattered.

Hot water from the shower fogs against the mirror while I strip out of my old clothes, leaving them lying on the bathroom floor.

Stepping under the water makes my body shudder.

I shower for a long time, letting the water caress over my body and thinking about the way Rufino's hands would brush against my skin.

My heart is in pain, overwhelmed with anguish - unfulfilled yearning for a man I don't know if I will ever see again.

Powerless, I crumpled to the ground, my legs unable to support me under the force of the spray.

I wrap my knees up against my chest and let my tears flow. The depth of my solitude is breaking me apart. My heart is shattering into smaller pieces with each passing day.

Where is he?

Nothing in this world makes sense without him.

After the shower I thought I would feel better, but I don't.

Wet hair hangs over my shoulders. I'm standing with my forehead against the window, looking down towards the ground - seventeen stories looks high enough to end this misery.

I press the palm of my hand against the glass and lean my weight into it.

What's the point of being here if he isn't coming for me?

Wind outside the closed window whistles through a small gap in the frame. A high-pitched sound that agitates me.

I step back. Staring at the misty imprint of my palm of the otherwise clean glass.

He'll come for me. *He has to. I can't lose hope.*

He won't leave me here. He promised.

All I need to do is be patient and wait. And not lose my mind which is steadily happening.

A plate gets shoved through the slot in the door.

I stare at it for a long time then sigh.

Eat. Stay strong. Be ready for when he comes.

I pick it up and carry it over to the bed. I sit on the edge with the food on my lap I stare at it again - thinking about how much I've changed.

How the things I want in my life have shifted.

"He'll come for me." I sigh, picking up the plastic fork and twirling the pasta around it.

CHAPTER TWENTY-FOUR
Rufino

"Yes, I've got what you asked for." He nods, pushing his thick glasses up the bridge of his nose with his fat fingers. I always pictured hackers looking cool. Dressed in neon colors and sporting wild attitudes. But this guy looks like he belongs in a library. Or like he lives in his mother's basement which I'm sure he doesn't with the amount of money I paid for this information.

I eye him up and down, waiting.

Dresden leans over his computer and tugs something out of a slot in the black. Sitting up again, he hands me a flash drive.

"Are you sure this is everything?" I ask, staring down at the small black rectangle, no bigger than a lighter.

"Every single one of the properties he owns. Including several in trusts and several that he tried very hard to conceal from public knowledge. He even used faked names for some of them. But I got them all. I don't doubt it for a second." He looks smug. Proud of his work.

"Residential and commercial?" I ask, flipping the drive in my hand.

"What - do you think I'm an amateur?" he snorts. "*Everything* that Luca A'Vara owns. Like I said. Even his well-hidden crypto-assets and some questionable charity funds."

I slip the flash drive into my pocket.

"We transferred the balance to your account this morning. It's all there."

"I know." He smiles, a weird sort of inhumane smirk that doesn't reach his eyes. He gives me the creeps. Lookin at him is like having ants crawling over my skin.

It's a relief to walk out of his weird underground office. It's crowded with too much tech. There are too many flashing lights and flickering screens. It's claustrophobic in there and smells of stale cheese.

In my car I slot the flash drive into the console of my LCD screen on the dashboard. Double tapping the only icon that shows up I grin when it opens a list of addresses. It better be everything. But even if it's not - it's enough to cause a lot of issues for the man.

I scroll down the list then back to the top. There's a lot of property to burn.

A lot of fires to light.

He has a lot to lose.

But before I start my rampage, I will give him a chance to do the right thing.

My engine purrs as I pull away from the hackers building and drive deeper into the city.

I punch my finger against the LCD Screen again and a list of phone numbers comes up.

"A'Vara." I say and the list narrows down to two names.

Verity and Luca.

My heart constricts at the sight of her name. The letters that make up the shape of her - I pull my mouth tight and punch my finger against 'Luca'. The pain of not having her can't distract me. Not now. Not when I am so close to getting her back. I've tried to dial Verity's number too. Over and over again. It always goes straight to voicemail. Her phone hasn't been on since we left my mansion.

His line rings.

Luca's voice fills my car.

"Rufino Vece, I was wondering where you were and when I'd get a call from you." His dry, emotionless voice fills me with rage.

"This is your last chance Luca. Give my wife back to me or I will take things from you." I warn him.

"You can try - but the agreement I had with your brothers - not to *kill* you - that was a onetime thing. If I see you again, I will put a bullet between your eyes and savor the moment."

"Where is my wife?" I ask again ignoring the threat.

"Have a nice evening, Rufino."

The lines goes dead, and silence sits heavily on my shoulders.

He made his choice.

Now I will make mine. He can't say I didn't give him a chance.

I flick back two screens and the list of properties is back on my dashboard.

I guess I'm starting at the top and working my way down the list.

His commercial properties take the first position on the list.

That good. It will be a bigger loss for him.

More money. More annoyance.

It's going to be a long night of painting this town red.

Before I make my way to the industrial side of town, I stop at my storage unit. The trunk pops open with the click of a button, so I can load it with five-gallon cans of gas. Enough to fill the entire space. The more the merrier.

I tap my pocket checking to see if my new lighter is still there.

The reassuring shape of it shifts against my hand.

I'm ready.

Slamming the trunk closed I climb back into the car. The smell of gasoline is already creeping into the front area.

It's like an entire year has passed since I locked Verity in the trunk of this same car.

I chuckle, remembering how pissed off she was with me.

"I'm coming, little vixen." I whisper, pulling away from the storage unit. I tap the first address on the list and a map opens up to show me the best route.

Thirteen minutes. Closer than I expected.

My music blasts at full volume to silence my thoughts so that I'm not distracted, I arrive at the address in no time at all. The building is dark and closed up. It's an office of some kind. But not a normal office where normal people work. It's too undercover. Too dark and closed up. There is no logo or company name on the outside to welcome clients in.

I carry two bottles of gasoline with me towards the back of the building. My eyes scanning in every direction I'm on high alert. No one can stop me.

The climb up the fire escape isn't easy with my hands full, but I make it work, tossing the bottles onto the level above me before I pull myself up.

On the fourth floor, one from the top, I kick open a window and use my sleeve to bash the broken glass clear from the frame so that I can climb through it without cutting myself. An alarm blares from the ground floor below me somewhere. A blue light flashes into the black night. I have seven minutes before this party is no longer private. Seven minutes to get this done.

Inside I find myself in a filing room. Lots of paper. Paper burns.

I walk into the other room. Computers sit in long lines across cubicles of desk space.

I walk to the end of the room and then make my

way back, tilting the bottle of fuel and letting it splash across the carpet.

I pause when I see a glowing light coming from a room to my left.

Setting the bottles down on the ground I move to investigate.

It's a server room. The low hum of tech makes me think of Dresden.

I nod in approval towards the information he gave me. Without him I would still wonder what the hell to do. The servers are loud, and the static agitate my skin.

There is a shit load of information stored here.

I hope it's important, old man. I hope it hurts when you lose it all.

I pick up the bottles again and take a deep breath of the now familiar smell of accelerant.

It's the scent of anarchy.

The scent of hell I am about to unleash on his life. Building by building I will make my way through the list until he give me what I want.

I use one bottle of fuel to dose the carpets and the other I pour down the elevator shaft. Splashing it along the wooden support beams and smiling to myself.

It's going to be beautiful when fire consumes everything inside here.

Back out on the fire escape on the other side of the broken window I toss the empty bottles back into the building and slip my lighter out of my pocket.

I can smell gas on my hands.

I don't care.

A click.

A spark.

A flame.

I touch the flame to the edge of the window frame and gasoline ignites.

I watch the blue tongue lap over the floor, devouring along the wet trail of fuel.

The flames lick upward onto the paper and I duck below the wall beneath the broken glass as explosive fire shoots from the widow.

I laugh as heat burns over my back.

I should move. The second explosion will be bigger.

Grabbing the railing of the fire escape I don't bother with the stairs. I slide straight down the framework and onto the ground, landing hard and running the moment my feet touch the ground.

Another loud explosion blasts around me and the ground seems to shake beneath my feet.

The flames have engulfed the entire building.

A dragon, eating its way out from the inside. For a moment I stand looking up at it, flames glowing against the windows on the fourth floor where the servers are and beginning to creep through on the other floors - eating from the elevator shaft.

The ground floor foyer area is already burning.

I can't stay though.

The alarm is silent now, but they're already on their way.

And I have other appointments at other buildings across this city.

My tires skid on asphalt as I pull away.

I am so fucking alive right now. My heart is thundering against my ribs like a hawk trying to claw its way out. Music blares around me again and I slam my finger against the screen. The map changes, showing me the way to the next address on the list.

This one is a warehouse at the docks.

Once I've got inside, I pour gasoline over wooden crates. I don't know what's in them and I don't care. I don't care about any of it.

All I want is her, and he is soon going to regret not giving me that.

I work until the entire floor space reeks of combustible liquids. Waiting for my lighter, ready to burn it all to ash.

At the wide steel doors I crouch low on the ground and touch the little flame to the floor.

The blue flame runs across the narrow river of gasoline towards the crate.

As soon as it reaches the crates the size of the fire

triples, lapping outward, it triple again and again until the entire warehouse is a furnace.

Sweat drips down my temple and I run my hand through my hair, pushing it back, away from my eyes.

The heat is breathtaking.

Bright orange and red is dancing in the reflection of my eyes and for a moment I am mesmerized by it and lost in thought.

I hear a car pulling up nearby and snap out of it.

Move.

They are here.

I bolt down the alley way on the side of the burning warehouse and back towards my car.

I can't stop smiling.

I can't wait to see her again.

After tonight is over, he will have lost so much he will beg me to take her.

I drive away with my lights switched off until I reach the main road. Then I press my finger against the next address.

I'm familiar with this area.

It's filled with high rises, tall and expensive and painful to lose.

I'll see if I can disable to alarm and take my time on this one. I want to cover as many floors in gasoline as possible to ensure that the entire building burns to the ground before they can put it out.

A quick stop at the storage unit is required though. I need more gasoline. And my tool kit to cut the security wires.

CHAPTER TWENTY-FIVE
Verity

Outside my room I hear a loud commotion. A door slams. There is shouting and someone is seething with rage. I stand up, tense, ready for anything. Waiting for Rufino to come bursting through the door. Waiting for gun shots and screaming. He must be here. He's found me. He's come to rescue me.

I stand deadly still, tilting my ear towards the sounds.

But it's just my father's voice. He's yelling and swearing at the security guards. I can't make out too much of what he's saying but I hear the word fire.

I walk closer to the door, a little nervous, but eager to find out what's going. By flicking open the food slot and holding it there I can make out more of the conversation. My body is shaking. Adrenalin surging through me.

"It's him. Who the fuck else would it be." My father snarls.

Rufino.

"Sir, we are not sure. We arrived after the person had already escaped."

I hear a thud, and someone huffing, gasping for air. My father hit him. "I said it was fucking him. Don't fucking question me."

"Yes, sir." A muffled response.

What did he do?

Where is he?

There's the rhythmic thud of pacing footsteps. My father is walking up and down. I can picture him. He does it often. He'll be clenching his jaw and lifting his upper lip as he takes long strides across the floor. His fists will be tight balls at his sides.

"How the fuck are we going to stop him?" he screams a rhetorical question to no one at all. And no one answers him.

"What about the girl?" one of the security guards asks.

"What about her?" he snaps.

"Why don't you just give her to him? Isn't that what he wants?"

There is a deadly silence that follows the question and I half expect a gunshot to fire off. My father does not have a high tolerance for stupidity. Or retreat.

I hold my breath, but nothing happens. My heart is beating in my ears, it's deafening.

"Open the door. I think the girl *is* the answer." My father commands.

I step away from it, backing up against the wall. What does he want to do with me? I doubt he will give me up. His ego would never allow that. He would rather see me dead that back with Rufino because giving me back would mean losing to a man he hates.

I wonder what Rufino has done to make him so angry.

I bite back a smile at the thought.

He *is* keeping his promise.

He *is* coming for me.

But he better hurry if he's going to get here before something happens to me. The door flies open and bangs against the wall behind it.

Two men run in with guns pointed at me, followed by my father.

He looks pale.

He's worried which is unusual for him. Nothing gets under his skin. He thinks he's invincible.

Whatever is going on has him on edge.

I keep my lips pressed together, not saying a word, waiting for him to speak first. I need more information because I can decide what to do.

"Give her the phone." He snarls.

One man throws a phone onto the bed near me.

I look at it - then back at my father.

"Pick up the fucking phone." He screams.

A guard moves closer to me, his gun looking threatening.

My father is beyond angry. He looks like he's losing control.

Precious control.

There is no telling what he will do if he reaches that point.

I grab the phone, gripping it in my fingers and waiting to find out what I'm supposed to do with it.

"Your boyfriend is burning down my buildings. One by one. He's taken two already. You are going to help me put an end to his rampage."

I grin, unable to stop myself.

"My husband." I correct him, walking on the broken glass of his shattered ego.

He takes in a sharp breath and flexes his jaw open and closed like a lion getting ready to devour his prey.

He nods towards the guard standing near me.

The man slings his gun over his shoulder and steps close to me.

The punch comes out of nowhere and while I am certain the guy can hit much harder than that - it knocks me to the point of nausea. I collapse to the floor gasping for air.

My hands press into the carpet where I sit on my knees blinking to clear my vision. The phone is lying on the ground next to me.

"Do you have any more smart ass comments or are you ready to do as you're told?" My father asks, sneering down at me.

"What do you want?" I spit, thick threads of anxiety creeping beneath my skin.

"Call him. His number is on there. Put the phone on speaker and call him. No codes. No secret messages. You are going to tell him to stop."

"He won't listen to me. Why would he stop? He wants you to give me back to him. That's the only thing that will make him stop." I shake my head. His plan is stupid. It won't work.

"He will stop because you are going to be very

convincing, Verity." My father says with a false sense of calm in his voice.

"How?" I ask, not understanding what he wants me to do.

"You are going to explain to him you never loved him. That it was just a bit of fun. You never cared about him at all and you're bored with his obsession."

"No." I gasp in horror. "I can't do that."

The security guard grabs me around the throat and lifts me up into the air. My feet dangle free, kick back and forth. I gasp for breath but he's holding me too tightly. My lungs are burning, begging for oxygen.

The world starts to spin and fade before he lets me go. I drop to the floor, landing hard and twisting my ankle.

Tears run down my cheeks.

My father has lost his mind.

He's willing to kill me to get me to do what he wants.

"Dial." He snaps.

I lean over and pick up the phone.

With shaking fingers I scroll through until I find Rufino's number.

I don't want this to be the last conversation I have with him.

I've been dreaming of hearing his voice for so long now. Sprawled out on the bed for hours imaging the conversation we would have when we see each other again. I wanted to hear him - and I'm about to get that wish - but this *isn't* what I wanted.

I swallow hard and clear my throat. Pressing the phone against my ear when it rings.

"Put it on speaker you fucking idiot." The guard kicks me in my thigh.

I wince and switch to the speaker. Holding the phone in front of me I can't keep it steady.

All the men are watching me. Their eyes stabbing into me like thousands of needles.

"Luca." Rufino's voice sinks into my mind like honey. Rich and dark and raw.

I can't speak. I can't find my voice. How am I going to do this?

The guard kicks me again and I bite down.

There is no way out of this. My father's actions have made it clear. If you don't do this, you will be beaten to death.

"It's Verity." I whisper.

"Little vixen." "Are you ok? I've been searching for you. Every moment of every day. I haven't stopped looking."

My father nods towards me. The guard presses his gun against my head.

"You can stop looking, Rufino." I sigh.

"What?" He sounds confused. I don't blame him. "Why would I stop looking?"

"Because I'm over it. I'm - bored. Or whatever." I do my best to sound sincere, to not let the tears creep through in my voice, but they are there. Choking my words.

"I don't believe you." He snarls. The edge of darkness on his voice is deep.

"You should believe me. Did you really think that someone like you could keep a girl like me? I'm too good for you. You would never have been able to keep up with me, anyway."

I squeeze my eyes shut trying to deny my own words. I want to push my silent thoughts through the phone so that he can feel the truth in my heart instead of the bullshit I'm saying out loud. My hand shakes even more.

"Verity don't do this." He warns me. "Don't give up on us."

"There never was an *us*, Rufino. And there never will be. Stop whatever you are doing to find me. Give up. Let go. Move on with your life."

A sob escapes my lips, and the guard nudges his foot against my side. A warning. I'm slipping up.

My father gestures with his eyes towards the phone and mouths the words "Convince him, stupid girl."

But I'm crying too hard now and when I speak the pain in my voice is impossible to hide. What am I doing? I'm risking everything. I'm going to lose him forever.

I'd rather die than be without him.

The threats my father is weighing onto me mean nothing compared to the idea of being without Rufino.

"Red, I love you." I scream into the phone. "I love you, please find me."

"Grab the phone." My father screams and the guard kicks it out of my hand. It slides across the floor, skidding under the bed. One guard drops to his knees, scrambling to get it. Rufino is yelling, but I can't hear what he's saying.

"You stupid fucking bitch, I wish you had died with your mother." My father's words don't even hurt because I feel nothing for him.

"Get the fuck out there and find him. Do whatever it takes."

I open my mouth to scream again but a fist slams into the side of my head and the world spins towards darkness as pain shoots through me.

I gasp and choke, fighting to hold on, but I can't.

My cheeks hits the floor, and my eyes are too heavy to keep open.

Their angry voices fade away and coldness covers me like a thick blanket.

I sink into oblivion.

Hoping, wishing and believing that Red will find me.

CHAPTER TWENTY-SIX
Rufino

I'm loading the last canister of gasoline into my trunk when my phone rings in my back pocket.

I haul it out and stare at it with amusement.

Luca.

I chuckle.

I wonder if he's figured out yet that it's me. He would be foolish to think it was someone else.

I made myself clear the last time we spoke.

The grin on my face is wide and tainted with hate when I answer his call.

"Luca." I say coldly.

The silence confuses me. Scrunching my eyes narrow I listen closer.

Why isn't he speaking?

I hold my breath, waiting.

My heart stops when she speaks.

"It's Verity."

Her voice is life itself.

My body collapses inward when I hear her and I have to lean against the side of the car to steady myself.

She's speaking softly, as though she's far away. But it's her, and that's all that matters.

Blood pulses thick in my veins and I am dizzy with relief.

"Vixen. Are you ok? I've been searching for you. Every moment of every day. I haven't stopped looking." I stammer, wanting to make sure she knows that I never gave up and never would have.

My heart is running a million miles an hour. Her

father must have surrendered and set her free. *My plan worked.*

"You can stop looking, Rufino." She sighs, sounding annoyed, or angry. I can't tell which. She doesn't sound like herself though. Not the girl I know. That beautiful angel who lay in my arms.

"What?" It makes little sense. "Why would I stop looking?"

Is it because she's free? I'm about to ask her where she is so that I can come and get her.

"Because I'm over it. I'm - *bored*. Or whatever."

Her words slice through me.

A hot knife slipping through butter. They sliced effortlessly. My heart is sinking into the pit of my stomach, weighed down by unspeakable pain.

But I shake my head. It's not possible.

This can't be real.

Verity would never say that. Someone is manipulating her.

I know her better than anyone on this fucking planet and I *know* she wouldn't say these things.

"I don't believe you." I growl into the phone with pure hatred for whoever is making her do this.

"You should believe me. Did you really think that someone like you could keep a girl like me? I'm too good for you. You would never have been able to keep up with me, anyway."

She goes quiet.

I swallow hard.

I don't know what to say to make her stop lying to me.

I don't know how to end this nightmare.

It can't be real, but she sounds so sincere. So honest. Is this what our relationship has been all along?

Was she just trying to concur me and move on?

A game? A dare? A challenge? The thought of her using me, tears me apart. It is as though someone is pulling my skin away from my bones in thick layers. Piece by piece peeling it away while I scream in agony.

How can this be possible? How can this be true?

"Verity, don't do this." I say with intense warning in my voice. "Don't give up on us." If I can just see her, if she will talk to me face to face I can remind her of how we are together.

We will be together.

Destiny chose for us to be together.

"There never was an *us*, Rufino. And there never will be. Stop whatever you are doing to find me. Give up. Let go. Move on with your life."

A heartbreaking sob echoes through the line.

She's crying.

I knew it.

I fucking knew it wasn't real.

Is she in tears because she's frightened?

What the fuck is going on?

I press the phone harder against my ear trying to listen. She needs me and I can't find her.

I have to get to her. I need a clue. I need something to guide me.

"Red, I love you." I jump when she screams into the phone. "I love you, please find me."

"Grab the phone." Luca screams.

There is a thud and a scraping sound.

"You stupid fucking bitch, I wish you had died with your mother."

My heart shatters.

"Get the fuck out there and find him. Do whatever it takes."

There is chaos. Movement. Violence. Danger.

What are they doing to her?

I can barely breathe as I listen. Waiting. Every muscle in my body is tense.

I want to hear her voice again. I need to know that she is ok.

But the line goes dead and the intensity of my rage multiples by a thousand as I let out an ear shattering scream.

I throw my phone into my car and walk around the back to slam the trunk closed. The fires stirred him enough to fake a breakup call from my wife. Let's see what else they can do.

And he's coming for me by the sounds of things. Well - let him. I look forward to it.

Let's see how many more buildings he's willing to lose before he believes I will never stop.

"You fucking idiot." I slam my fists against the steering wheel, screaming at a man who can't hear me.

The sound of her crying has only made this worse for him. He made a mistake having her call me. It's pushed me deeper into my anarchy. It's made me set on making his life a living hell.

I click against the next building on the list.

Only eight minutes from where I am.

Perfect. The sooner I set it on fire, the sooner he will realize his mistake.

A seventeen story high rise in town, it must be worth a fortune.

I'll make sure every floor is a raging furnace that no one can extinguish. By the time morning comes, there will be nothing left but ash. Tires screech and burnt rubber spins in the air behind me when I take off.

I'll burn everything. I won't stop till morning. I'll get through so much of that list tonight that he'll have almost nothing when the sun rises.

Outside the building I come face to face with security which doesn't surprise me. He knows I'm coming. He would have tried to secure his most important properties. I guess this one is a favorite.

The men don't stand a chance against me though. They have no idea of the darkness festering in my heart. The pure rage I'm carrying for the man they are working for.

Their bodies litter the foyer and the elevator by the time I've cleared the first level.

I move, carrying all the bottles of gasoline into the elevator. Pressing every button on the panel I set it to stop on every floor.

At the start of each passageway I kick a bottle of fuel over, sending it skidding down the passage and flooding gasoline over the floor.

Level by level I make my way to the top floor.

I'll coat the seventeenth floor from top to bottom and set it alight before I head back down, sparking each floor as I descend.

He's pushed me too far. But soon he'll see his mistake in underestimating me.

The elevator chimes on the seventeenth floor and I climb out carrying two bottles, their caps already off, I walk to the farthest end of the long passage, passing doors as I go. When I walk past I splash fuel against the doors and walls, letting it soak into the carpet.

Half way down the passage back towards the elevator I can barely breathe for the stench. It's burning my eyes and my lungs. Making it hard to focus.

I'm taking too long.

If I don't get out of here soon he'll arrive with more forces and I won't live to see it burn. I'm sure those other guards must have alerted them to my arrival here. Not that I gave them a lot of time. But there is still a chance they got a message through to him.

Down the passage I hear a thump and turn to see a guard come thundering through the door right at the end of the hallway.

"Fuck." I mutter. Not keen on being delayed anymore.

Two more come running at me from behind. They must have come up the elevator while I was busy pouring the gasoline.

"Fuck." I scream again in frustration.

I acted blindly and ignored everything around me.

I won't let them kill me though - if they do I am taking this entire building with me.

I kick the bottle of gasoline over and watch the clear liquid splash out in a thick flood.

Lifting my hand over my mouth to block out some of the sharp stench I pull my gun from the holster and fire two shots towards the guards running down from the elevator.

My aim is brilliant and they both collapse to the ground. My gun clicks empty. The barrel sitting open to let me know I'm out of bullets and out of luck.

The other guard, coming at me from the end of the hallway - he reaches me faster than expected and slams into my back before I face him, knocking me to the ground. I roll sideways and avoid soaking myself in fuel, but he isn't so lucky.

He swears and rolls again, drenching himself even more.

The darkest smile touches my lips as I flick the lighter to life.

The flame becomes a beacon of my rage.

"What the fuck?" he scream as I throw it at him.

It hits him in slow motion and the flames cover him like a strait jacket, wrapping around every inch of his body.

He staggers backwards, falling to the floor, rolling and screaming and trying to put himself out, but all he's doing is moving towards where I've soaked the hallway.

When his burning body touches against the carpet near the back of the passage it's a glorious sight.

The explosion knocks me off my feet and I

scamper away from the wave of heat that slams into me.

Touching my face to check if it's singed my hair off.

It hasn't. But sweat is pouring of me.

The entire back end of the hallway is raging red, orange and blue.

The fire roars with anger, spreading.

I have to leave.

Now.

I should never have set it alight while I was still so far inside the building.

But it's so beautiful. The destruction.

For a second I'm lost in the sheer power of it, watching the flames spread like a virus ready to take over every inch of this place.

Move, dammit, Red. Or you'll die here.

Grinning, I turn to run towards the elevator - but freeze in place.

The scream that shatters through the seventeenth floor sends a shudder of pain through me. I know who it is. I just know.

"Verity?" I shout down the passage, but an explosion drowns out my voice as one of the side doors caves in "Verity." I shout again.

Another scream carries to me from the far end of the passage.

No.

What have I have done?

I run straight into the uncontrollable furnace of death. Ducking low to save myself from the heat and smoke suffocating my lungs and stinging my eyes.

"Verity." I shout again, but there is no answer.

At the end of the hallway I can hardly see anything.

I kick against the only door there.

I kick until it crumples in on itself.

"Verity." My voice is just a dry whisper now and

when I take in a breath to try to sooth it I choke on thick grey smoke.

Dropping to the ground I leopard crawl into an apartment.

It doesn't make sense. Why is there an apartment here?

CHAPTER TWENTY-SEVEN
Verity

I n my dreams I'm running.

It's so hot my skin is being scorched by the air around me as the sun blisters down from above.

I lift my hand up over my face and squint into the distance. Rolling red desert hills surround me from every angle. I've been walking for eternity. My throat is screaming for water, cracked and dry, aching to the point where I can't speak anymore.

I pull the soft white fabric up over my face, but it does nothing to block out the heat of the sun above me. I'm trapped here, but I don't remember how I got here.

I'm scared, but I don't know which way to go. Everywhere

I've walked so far is just more sand. More hills. More painful, blistering heat.

My skin is burnt and red and my body is ready to quit.

I can't stop though. If I stop I will die. I've got to keep moving.

But my feet are too heavy to lift, and when I look down, I see the sand wrapping around my legs - I'm in a sink hole. The sand is reaching up to embrace me in its fiery tomb.

I'm too hot.

I have to get away. But there isn't anywhere to go.

The sand sucks me deeper into the ground and the more I fight the quicker I sink.

It's up around my throat and I'm twisting, lifting my head, trying to take one last breath of air.

Terror has taken over.

I'm about to die. There is no escape. My mind knows it, even though my body is desperate to fight until the last second.

It's inevitable. My death.

But I don't want to die.

I scream.

But when I open my mouth sand pours down my throat, straight into my lungs.

Red, hot, desert sand that seers my insides and wraps around my outsides like a clay furnace, roasting against my skin.

I wake up choking on imaginary desert sand, gagging and heaving to get it out of my throat. The more I breathe in the worse it gets.

Sitting up on the bed I realize the air is thick with grey smoke.

It's not sand I'm choking on.

Its smoke.

I roll off the bed and land with a thud on the floor.

My head hurts. I can feel a throbbing point in my temple where that asshole punched me unconscious, but right now it seems like the least of my worries.

As I scoot underneath the bed, I try to remember

what happened, but I can't figure out why the entire room is engulfed in smoke.

The door is still closed. Where is everyone? Why didn't the guards let me out of here?

I leopard crawl across the floor to the door, rolling onto my back I kick against it and shouting for whoever is there to let me out. No one answers and the door doesn't budge.

Reaching up I push the food slot open to look through, but the brass metal is so hot it burns my skin and I wince, yanking my hand back to my side.

"Fuck." I say breathlessly.

If I can make it to the window, I can try to break the glass.

I need air.

I'm so desperate for air.

My eyes are watering so much I can barely see the surrounding room.

I crawl out from the door towards the window and heat from above scorches down on me. It's too hot. I'm too scared.

I'm going to die here.

For a moment I'm frozen in place and waiting for death. Paralyzed by the inevitable.

Fuck that. I'm won't give up like that.

Rufino is coming for me. I know he is. All I have to do is survive until he does.

I belly crawl towards the window, but half way across the carpet a massive explosion sounds from somewhere nearby. I let out an ear-piercing scream of fear and rage. Determination to live and the terror of dying.

Part of the ceiling caves in and flames spread across the dry plaster.

I roll onto my back and look up at the water stained dragon, being licked by beautiful orange tongues, devoured piece by piece and turning black.

Destruction.

Beautiful, unrestrained destruction.

And soon my body will meet the same fate.

There will be nothing left of me to find. Nothing but a charred outline of who I once was.

I roll back onto my stomach and start crawling towards the window again.

Another part of the ceiling caves in and a chunk of plaster falls to the ground, landing right next to me. I roll away from me, gasping in fright and letting out another death wrenching scream.

I'm hit with a coughing fit when dry, hot smoke streams into my lungs.

Inch by inch I won't give up, I'll keep going.

My fingers tear into the carpet as I pull myself forward. But my body is giving up. It's like quick sand.

I'm too heavy to move and I no long have enough air to breathe.

I'm right beneath the window. It's right there.

Please, Verity. You're stronger than this. You can do this.

Get up.

Grab the chair.

Throw it at the glass.

My eyes squeeze shut, and my panicked thoughts run wild.

Focus.

One thought.

One plan.

Nothing else matters but that.

I push myself up onto my knees and it feels like I'm trying to lift the weight of the world on my shoulders. I have to fight my own instincts. The ones telling me to take deeper breaths. To gasp and flood my lungs with life - because it won't be life. It will be certain death.

Lifting my t-shirt up over my mouth the thin fabric does nothing to ease the burn of the smoke. My mouth tastes like smoke. My lips are charred and cracked. My skin feels like it's melting off my body.

I reach out to grab the chair, sitting on my haunches to stay low from the flames above my head.

I pick the chair up with great effort and holding my breath I swing it towards the window with every ounce of energy I have left inside me.

It thumps against the glass and ricochets back at me.

But the glass doesn't shatter.

It doesn't even crack.

I'm lying on my back again and this time I can't get up. My body no longer responds when I tell it to fight.

Another piece of the ceiling caves in and lands on the bed where I was lying unconscious only moments ago.

I'm going to die in here.

And all I can think about is him.

I'm so sorry, my beautiful Viking. I'm so that I couldn't see you again. I'm sorry I wasn't strong enough to fight these flames.

I roll onto my side, trying to get closer to the wall beneath the window.

But this is it. This is as close as I'm getting.

I can't move anymore.

I can't even breathe.

"Rufino." A dry, cracked whisper flaking off my lips. But I want the last thing I hear to be his name. "Rufino." I say again, but it doesn't even sound like a word anymore.

CHAPTER TWENTY-EIGHT
Rufino

I crawl inside the once modern and neat apartment, searching everywhere for her. The living room is turning black while smoke rubs against the walls and ceiling. A layer of ash coats the sofa, drifting like snowflakes from above where the ceiling is on fire.

"Verity." I scream her name again but there is no answer.

I heard her. She has to be in here somewhere.

Standing up I run from room to room. A small kitchen engulfed in flames. I can't even step inside it because the wall of heat is too much. But she's not in there, anyway.

The bathroom is crumbling inward. The shower is filled with shattered glass after part of the ceiling crashed down.

In a back room I find what I'm looking for.

There is a guard crouched low on the ground, struggling to breathe as he leans against a heavy locked door. The security on the door tells me it's a holding cell. Verity has to be trapped in there. Her father was using this safe house as her prison and I set it all on fire.

My blood boils as I draw the knife from my ankle strap and approach the guard.

The anger burns within me for putting Verity in such a dangerous situation.

I'm angry because I don't know if she's still alive.

I'm angry because if I killed her, if I hurt her - I will never forgive myself.

The guard mumbles something, his eyes are bloodshot and watering. He clutches at his throat then in shock he sees me crouched in front of him.

He tries to reach for the gun lying on the floor at

his side, but his movements are heavy and uncoordinated.

I lean towards him and with one swift arch of my arm I shove the knife through is lower jaw, up into his skull before he screams.

His body twitches as blood runs over the handle of the knife, down the front of his shirt. I kick his body out of the way so that I can open the door.

I hear her coughing from behind the secured door.

I've got to get in there now.

Panic takes over and I search the guards dead body for the key. If I can't find it, I will shoot the locks off, but I fear hitting her with a stray bullet. I don't know where she is on the other side. She could be leaning right up against the door the same way the guard was.

Relief soaks through me when my fingers touch the keys inside the pocket of his jacket.

I grab them, the metal is hot in my hands while I search for the right one.

When I get it I shove it into the first lock. My eyes are watering so much it's hard to see. I get the second lock open and shove my body weight against the door.

It opens easily. She isn't close by.

I squint towards a bed, fear surges when I see the ceiling has collapsed onto it and the bedding is on fire beneath thick chunks of burning plaster.

In blind panic I run to the bed and start pulling the ceiling board off it. Searching for her. Grabbing at burning blankets, the coals, and flames bite into my skin. Salty sweat is dripping into my eyes.

My skin is charring, dry and hot.

The smoke is thicker in here and my lungs are screaming for air.

Squinting against the grey veil.

Thick red flames are dancing on the ceiling and up the walls.

If she was on the bed when the ceiling fell - she will be dead.

Verity will be dead.

My search turns to rage as I kick the bed and send

the last pieces of wood splintering across the floor towards another door.

Another door.

I run towards that, but my legs buckle beneath me.

I'm dying.

My body is breaking apart with lack of oxygen and overwhelming heat.

Pushing myself up again I move slower. I can't save her if I kill myself first.

The handle is too hot to touch so I kick it and when it flies open flames shoot out of the bathroom, searching for oxygen in this room.

That's what happens when you open a window into a burning room. Oxygen pours in, which you are desperate for, but all it does is feed the fire.

Verity is not in here either.

This is impossible. She has to be somewhere.

"Verity." I scream again, staying low and hunched, keeping my head beneath the building layer of smoke over the ceiling.

Back in the other room I see a chair, toppled over near the window.

And then I see her.

Verity is lying on the floor beneath the window. Her body is still. Lifeless.

"No." I shout, standing up and running to her. Ignoring the pain in my lungs and the fire licking at my skin.

"No."

I collapse onto the floor next to her and roll her onto her back so that I can see her face.

I can't tell if she's breathing.

There's no time.

I must get her out of here before if it's too late - if it isn't already.

Lifting her in my arms I cradle her against my chest and move towards the door.

As I walk through it part of the frame collapses and a chunk of burning wood smacks into my face. I turn my head just in time for it to only hit my cheek and not my eye.

I can't even feel it.

I can't feel anything anymore except for the anguish of losing her.

I run, stumble and get up, carrying her out of the apartment and into the hallway.

It is a tunnel of death.

An endless pipe of fire resembling the belly of a snake, or a dragon -

I can't do this.

I have to do this.

Glancing down at her face, her cheeks black with soot and her lips so dry and flaked - I have a renewed sense of urgency and determination.

My beautiful wife.

I have found you.

I have killed you.

With a guttural scream of rage and hope and fear and hate and determination - I run.

Shielding her with my arms, turning my body into the flames - I run.

The other side of the building closer to the elevator is not burning as severely.

The fire has not reached here yet and I thank every star in the entire galaxy when I see the elevator is still open and waiting for me.

Inside I take desperate breaths of air. It's still hot. Muggy. Smokey. But it's air. Better than what I was breathing before.

I am close to death, but I know she is closer.

Punching my finger against the G, I step deeper into the elevator and crouch onto my knee, resting her on the ground.

"Verity." I say, touching her face.

"Verity don't do this. Don't give up. I'm so sorry."

Her chest is moving.

Her eyes are dancing beneath closed lids as though she was dreaming.

"Verity." I scream louder.

The elevator doors close, and I stare down the passage, disintegrating faster and faster as the flames lick towards us.

Another explosion shakes the elevator just as the doors close and it jolts, slipping on the cable that's holding us seventeen stories above the ground.

I grab Verity into my arms again and hold her cradled against my chest.

We move and another explosion shakes the building.

The fire has dripped through the floor boards and onto each level below. Levels I tipped bottles of gasoline into.

As we pass one floor, a flame touches one of those bottles and the explosion smacks up against the metal doors.

I turn my body away from the doors and the heat of it blasts against my back. The cable slips again and we plunge into free fall.

I bury my face in her ash covered hair and whisper "I love you."

She moans softly.

My heart races. We are falling to our death.

The elevator jerks as it tilts to the side and gets wedged between the walls of the shaft.

One cable has snapped. The other is holding us by a thread.

One wrong movement and we will plummet to our deaths.

Verity moans and shifts in my arms.

"Verity." I call her name, desperation dripping from my voice. "Please be ok." I beg her.

"Rufino." An aching whisper of hope. "Are you really here?" She chokes, coughing dry ash.

I laugh, tears streaming over my ashen skin.

"I'm here. I'm real."

She shakes her head and reaches her hand up to touch her throat.

"I'm dreaming." Her voice rustles like dried leaves dancing in a soft breeze.

"Yes, my love. This is a dream. When you wake up, you'll be somewhere safe. I promise you. I'll get us out of here."

Above us, right in the elevator shaft, another explosion takes place, and the force drives the metal box we are trapped in harder against the walls.

We will not fall any further, but we are not going to able to get to the ground this way anymore.

Setting Verity on the tilted floor of the elevator I scramble up towards the doors, one is bent and ever so slight open. I pry my fingers into the gap and scream with effort as I pull it apart. At first it won't move. Stuck. Trapping us in a metal oven of certain death.

I glance over my shoulder at Verity. She is unconscious again.

I will get her out of here.

I pull again, my muscles strain and flex and scream until the door shifts and slides open. Just enough for us to get out.

Moving quickly, I scoop her into my arms and lift her out through the crack.

We are stuck half way between one of the floors. I have no idea how far we fell and how many levels we are above the ground.

I have to lift her up over my shoulders to glide her body onto the floor.

She moans and sparks glitter above our heads. I duck down with fright. The elevator shifts. Perhaps it is not as stable as I thought.

Verity is out, lying on the carpet. Breathing gently.

I reach up and grab the edge of the floor, pulling myself up onto it.

Kicking my legs through the elevator shifts again and another explosion somewhere above us makes it shudder and move.

I scream, pulling myself the last few inches through the door just as it breaks free of the wall and starts falling again.

A gust of air whips over us as it sucks the elevator down.

I close my eyes, counting the seconds until I hear the loud, shattering crash as it smashes into the ground floor.

Six.

Six seconds.

Which means we are six floors from the ground.

I hear the loud rumble before I realize what's happening.

A ball of fire is rushing down the open elevator shaft as fresh oxygen rushes from the ground upwards to greet the flames on the top floors.

They transformed it into a giant flame thrower.

The sound is deafening.

I roll over her, my body covering her as flames blast from the partially open doors.

They spit in a thick stream above my head.

My jacket is on fire. I can feel it scratching my skin.

"Rufino." She screams beneath me.

"Don't move." I scream back.

When the fire pulls back into the shaft I roll off her, onto my back to smother the flames.

I'm hurting everywhere. But I don't care.

Verity tries to sit up, but she can hardly move.

She rolls onto her side, coughing, and spitting ash.

I pull her into my arms.

"I'm going to get us out of here." I say. "I'll get us out."

CHAPTER TWENTY-NINE
Verity

He pulls me into his arms, and I can't believe it's him.

I'm struggling to hold on to consciousness, but desperate to know if this is real or just another dream.

I look up into his face, dark with ash and dirt. His cheek is bleeding and looks burnt with agony. I touch my fingers against it, and he winces.

"Sorry." I whisper. And he laughs.

"What's so funny?" I whisper, my throat aches.

"You have nothing to be sorry for. *I'm* sorry. *I'm so fucking sorry.*" He says his voice tight with regret and shame.

I scrunch my eyes. "Why? You came to save me."

"I did this, Verity. I set the building on fire. I put your life at risk."

My chest is aching. My lungs hurt. My eyes are burning, and every part of my body is in excruciating pain.

But I smile as I close my eyes again.

"Why are you smiling?" his voice sounds far away.

"You burned the world down for me." I whisper. And the world sinks away from me. But I know I'm in his arms, so I don't care. I don't care about anything but him. He's here.

He burned the world down for me.

I feel him lift my body, limp and heavy, into his arms.

"I'm going to get us out of here, vixen." His voice touches the edges of my dream.

I'm being carried on the shoulders of a massive beast. He keeps talking to me, but I don't understand the soothing words that are coming from his lips. It's garbled and makes little sense. I struggle to hear over the loud rumble growling in the distance. Something dangerous is following us. Something big is creeping towards us and I'm terrified, but the beast is gripping me.

He jogs, and my body jolts against his broad shoulders, his arm wrapped over my back to keep me from falling off.

Sometimes when I try to take a breath into my lungs, it tastes of thick ash and I cough.

The beast pauses. Talking to me again.

I wish I knew what he was saying.

His words have the power to enchant me and transport me to a world of magic and wonder.

I open my eyes and flames above my head lick down towards my face.

I cry out in fright and Rufino digs his fingers into my side.

"It's ok, Verity. We're on the fourth floor now. We're so close to the ground. We're almost out of here."

"Rufino." I gasp, my words huff from my chest when he moves, and I get shifted against his shoulder. He is carrying me fireman style, slung over his shoulder, shifting on his back.

I groan. Breathing hurts.

I close my eyes and feel my head dropping.

My arms go limp and my body slumps down.

The beast shouts when a massive dragon leaps from behind a rock and blasts a tongue of fire towards us. He ducks and rolls and I fall from his shoulders. The dragon rears up, screeching a high-pitched whine and then a low rumble of anger.

This is what we were running from - and now it's found us.

We are going to die.

"Ugh." Rufino grunts as he lifts me back up and onto his shoulders.

To our left a room is blazing and the door from that room is lying splintered and covered in flames just in front of us.

"Ruf—" I try to say his name, but I can't. A coughing fit steals my breath away and I fight for air as he jogs towards the stairwell.

"Three more floors, my love. We are almost there. We are almost safe." He says, straining and sounding like he's in pain as well.

"Ruf—"

My eyes burn and my head drops.

The dragon is right behind us, slinking over the ground, slithering and creeping and following everywhere we go.

Tears are streaming down my cheeks.

I don't want to die like this.

I don't want to die at all.

How can I help the beast? He is in pain and I want to help him somehow. But when I try to move but my body isn't working. My legs are too heavy, weighed down like iron, my arms are limp and useless. I can't even reach up to grip against the beast's shoulder.

My heart aches for him.

This monster carrying me.

This terrifying creature that would strike fear into the heart of any person who looked upon him. But my heart is with him. He owns me. He has me. I belong to him and no one else.

Nothing can pull us apart. Not even the dragon lurking close on our heels.

A loud crash vibrates into my dream and snaps me awake.

I cry out fear. "The dragon."

Behind me the roof caves in and a dark flames spike through the air.

The smoke has turned black and I can't see in front of us.

"Hold on, my love." He screams over the roar of fire and the sounds of the building caving in around us. "I can see the exit. It's blocked but I'll find a way. Just hold on."

I dig my fingers into his back. Attempting to hold on to him, my hands fail me, and my mind falters once more.

The dragon is snapping at my feet. His massive reptilian jaws and opening and closing with a force that sends a shockwave pushing past me. I scream and the sound vibrates against the beast's back.

He speaks to me. Reassurance. Soothing calm.

I still can't understand him.

He runs and jumps, and I am pushed and shaken and

jolted and in so much pain I don't know if I can last much longer.

But in front of us I see a wall of ice.

Crystal clear. Bright.

I know that if we reach that wall we will be ok.

The dragon's fire can't break through the ice.

"Run." I scream. As the dragon leaps towards us and his teeth cut across my leg. "Run. Please, run." I beg.

The beast pushes with everything he has inside him. His fingers grip me it feels like his hands will tear my skin away.

He runs.

He runs like the rushing water of a tidal wave, shoving things out of his path and leaping over long rips in the earth's surface. He jumps over rocks and fallen trees. He runs to save us.

Straight towards the wall of ice.

Bright and blue and safe.

As we get closer, I look up and see that it isn't ice as all but a shimmering silver liquid. It glitters and pulses like water.

He doesn't slow down, and I squeeze my eyes shut, not knowing what will happen when he crashes into it. Not knowing if I'm right. If that is what will save us. Or if it's just a trick. A trap. Another way to die.

As the glittering liquid wall slams into us an icy coldness coats my skin and the contrast of it, compared to the dragons flames, is so painful that again I find I can't breathe.

The shift in temperate is like a blade across my skin.

I'm drowning in silver snow. It floods into my lungs and I can't stop coughing.

Gasping and choking as spears cut the inside of my lungs.

I feel my body being lifted of the beasts shoulders and laid down onto the cold, damp ground.

"Verity - "

I know that name.

"Verity."

It's my name.

I blink my eyes open and my vision is too blurry to make out where I am. Cold, crisp air pours into my lungs.

"Verity, can you hear me?" Rufino's voice pulls me from my dreams again.

"I - " I choke.

"Oh thank fuck. Oh my fuck - " he mutters. Pulling me up against his chest. "I thought I lost you." He growls against my ear.

I reach up and rub my eyes, blinking again and again until the tears and gone.

Fresh, chilly night air is touching my skin.

It hurts.

My skin is too sensitive, and my lungs are filled with needles.

"I - I'm alive - " I mutter.

He laughs. "You're alive."

Above us something explodes, and he grunts in fright.

"We're still too close. My car is just around the corner." He mutters, sliding his arm around my back and lifting me against his chest he runs.

I cry out in pain as his movements shoot through me.

"Hold on, my love."

Looking back, I see the building fall.

The top floors caving in, level by level, a loud rumbling, crumbling monster.

"A dragon." I whisper.

As it collapses sparks and flames glitter into the dark night and thick streams of black smoke pour into the sky.

"It's a dragon." I mumble again and then collapse against him.

I feel the darkness more than I can see it.

In fact, I can't see anything.

I can't even see my hand when I hold it right in front of my face.

"Where am I?" I mutter and my voice doesn't seem to go anywhere. It's as though the darkness absorbs the sound as soon as it leaves my lips.

The ground beneath my feet vibrates and I crouch low to steady myself.

I wish I could see.

I wish I knew what was happening.

It sounds like an engine. Like I'm inside something, growling and rumbling as it carries me towards the unknown.

I spin in a circle, remembering the dragon, searching for it in a moment of fear. However, there is nothing.

The dragon is lost somewhere behind us.

I was with someone.

The beast.

"Beast?" I scream as loud as I can. But once more, the blackness swallows the sound. Muffled and lost and unheard.

I feel his hand on my thigh, squeezing gently.

"We're almost at the hospital, little vixen. You're so strong. Keep fighting."

A loud screech of car tires skid against the tarred road as he takes a corner at incredible speed. My body rolls to the left and he grabs me, pulling me back into my seat.

I want to tell him everything in my heart.

I want to tell him how I feel.

But I can't speak. My throat is too tight, too dry.

My eyes are too heavy. Burning from dry air and smoke.

I sigh, and even that grates against the burnt skin of my larynx, aching.

Closing my eyes I feel my body slump forwards. I can't even hold myself up.

My flops down onto something hard. I blink up into bright, glaring white lights. "Where - " I mutter. Then swallow away the pain.

"Hello, sweetie, my name is Lisa, I'm a nurse. You're at the Swan Hospital. Can you tell me your name?"

"Rufino - " I mutter again.

"Is that the man who brought you in?"

"Ruf—" his face appears above me. We are moving fast down a long white passage. People are shouting and calling out distinct orders.

"I'm right there, my love. I'm here. You're safe."

I close my eyes and the weight of my head

becomes too much to bare. It lulls to the side, my cheek pressing against something soft.

"She's losing consciousness again. We need to hurry."

"Is she going to be ok?"

"Sir, please, you need to step back and let us do our jobs."

A loud beeping piercings through the darkness of my mind.

I'm sitting on the ground. It's soft beneath me but I still can't see anything. I can't say anything because it falls to nothing when it leaves my lips.

And my throat aches.

No one can hear me, and no one knows I'm here.

Maybe they do. Maybe they're searching for me, but they are just as lost as I am.

I gave up walking because I don't know if I'm getting anywhere.

So now I'm just waiting.

I sigh. A blunt sound. Muffled.

I wish he was with me.

If he was here, I wouldn't be so alone and empty.

He promised to burn the world down for me.

He promised to tear it apart if he ever lost me.

My heart pulls tight in my chest.

"Rufino." I say, soundless and silent. "My Viking."

CHAPTER THIRTY
Rufino

I haven't left the hospital for two days. Verity is still unconscious, and I'm terrified she will never wake up.

I'm completely drained and barely functioning without adequate rest, food, or anything else. I can't focus on anything but her.

The smoke damage to her lungs was bad. They had her on a ventilator, pumping oxygen into her system for almost a full twenty-four hours before they were confident enough to take her off it.

Now she is on a drip and a cocktail of painkillers.

Between the dehydration and the smoke she is in

not in a good way and they can't tell me when—or if—she will wake up.

It's killing me to not know.

Somehow I made it out in better shape than her. Which isn't saying much.

I am in a great deal of pain. Every part of my body is pain. My have bruises all over, my lungs are heavy, and it's hard to breathe, my skin is red and sensitive to touch. My face now sports a long, aching scar from just above my right eye all the way down my cheek.

My face is half burnt, half cut. A thin row of stitches hold the skin closed.

Will she still love me when she sees me like this?

Will she still love me when she realizes I am the one who caused her all of this pain?

The doctors have tried to give me painkillers as well but I don't feel that I deserve them after what I did. I deserve to be in pain. I deserve to be hurting. My body and my heart.

I don't know if I even deserve to be with Verity anymore.

But I can't let her go. I can't give up on our love.

I've been sitting too long. Staring at her resting face. Sometimes she mutters in her sleep, wordless panic as she fights imaginary things. Fire. Heat. Pain. Smoke.

She scrunches her nose and knots her brows and tosses in her lost space - lock up inside her own mind. I talk to her and she quietens down, other times my voice makes her panic worse.

I am helpless. But not hopeless.

If I lose hope that she will come back to me then I've lost the will to live.

In moments of peace, she seems joyful, as if she could stay lost in her own mind forever.

I talk to her to remind her I love her and I want her back. I tell her not to give up.

The hospital chairs are uncomfortable. Everything is uncomfortable.

I need to move so I stand up and pace up and down along the hospital passage outside her private room. Not far away. I want to be here when she opens her eyes. I want to be the first thing she sees.

But I can't take the constant, methodical beep of her heart monitor because I've become so fixated on it - and terrified it will come to a sudden stop.

It's taunting me and I listen to it for hours with intense fear growing inside me.

I'm driving myself insane. Sick to my stomach.

I've never felt this stressed in my entire life.

I can't lose her.

And I can't live with myself if I am the one who killed her.

"Is she awake yet?" I turn towards my brother's voice - a tight knot forming in my stomach. Masaccio is standing in the hospital passage with a take away coffee in his hand. "Here - this is for you. Thought you might need it." His other hand is shoved into his pocket and he doesn't appear to be confrontational in any sense, but I never know with him. Sometimes he tries to manipulate me with the pretense of calm.

"What are you doing here?" I snarl, not at all interested in any lectures right now. If he's here to tell me I fucked up–he can save it. I'm not in a listening mood.

"Just came to see how you were doing." He shrugs, putting the coffee down on a little table nearby.

I look at it for a while. I really need a coffee, but I can't tell if it's a gesture of peace or not. Whatever. It's coffee. It smells amazing.

Picking it up, I shake my head. "She hasn't woken up yet. I'm losing my mind waiting."

"I'm sorry to hear that." He sighs. "She's a strong girl though. I'm sure she will be fine."

I sip the coffee, savoring the dark sweet taste for a moment. Then I sigh and clench my jaw. Let's just get straight to the point.

"Mas, just tell me why you're really here so we can get this over with."

He pulls his mouth tight and sets his eyes on me. "We were all worried about you. Everyone wanted to come down and see you, especially Dalila. She threw a flat out tantrum when I asked her not too, for now - I asked them to let me come alone - uh - just to smooth things out first. I came to say that I'm sorry for the way we handled things."

I study him carefully, looking for any signs of insincerity, but finding none.

My eyes trace over the cut on his cheek. It's not bad. When it heals, you won't even see the scar. But I still feel bad about it.

"Ok." I reply.

His shifts his weight from one foot to the other.

The awkward silence between us is made worse by the fact that I know I need to apologize too.

"Alright then." Masaccio says with a soft smile. "I'll head out. But if you need anything, let me know." He turns to walk away. "And I'll tell our sister she can come visit if she wants to."

"Wait." I huff.

Stopping, he glances over his shoulder.

"Is Tuomo ok?" My feet shift awkwardly this time and I suddenly don't know what to do with my other hand so I shove it into my pocket too.

"He's a bit pissed off, but he's ok." Mas chuckles, gingerly touching his own cheek. "It'll all blow over, Red. We're family. We fight. We make up. Don't worry about it."

I nod, biting the inside of my cheek.

"I'm sorry - about all of that. I am not sorry for fighting to win her back - but I am regretful about the other things."

Mas turns to face me. "Do you know what your new nickname is on the streets? Have you heard what they're calling you?"

"No?" I scrunch my brows. I've been out of the loop for far too long now. Consumed with getting Verity back and not interested in anything else.

He laughs. "They call you The Red Dragon. I like it. Sounds ominous. And you earned it." He raises his brows. News about the fires is spreading.

"I guess I did." I grin.

Mas turns his back on me again. "Let us know when she wakes up."

"Sure."

My brother walks away from me, headed out of the hospital. I appreciate his effort to come here and resolve the situation. It was bothering me. I don't always get on with my family, but I don't want to be at war with them.

"Sir - come quickly she might be waking up."

I bolt towards her room, almost knocking the nurse over. I'm at her bedside in a matter of seconds.

Taking her hand, I whisper her name.

"Verity, vixen."

She sighs and groans a bit before her eyes flicker.

Patience was never my strong point, but I'm trying - trying not to grab her into my arms or flood her with everything that's in my heart before she's awake.

"Red." She whispers - that gorgeous smile touching the edges of her lips.

"Hey you." I grin. "Welcome back."

"How long - has - it?"

"You've been resting for almost three days."

The nurse standing on the other side of her bed holds out a glass of water. "Here you go sweetie. Let's lift your bed so you can drink a little."

The bed hums as it tilts upward.

I wait while the nurses check her over and make sure she's ok.

When we are alone, I pull a chair next to her bed and sit down, taking her hand in mine.

"Verity, I need to tell you how sorry I am for what I did to you."

"What do you mean?"

"The fire - I almost killed—"

"Stop." She demands. "Red, don't you get it? You promised to burn the world down until you found me and - you did. You did all of that for me. You set me free. I fucking love you." She grabs the collar of my shirt and tugs me towards her.

She doesn't have to ask twice. I stand up and lean over her, pressing my lips against her and kissing her.

Something I've been longing to do for far too long.

Lying down next to her on the hospital bed, she wraps her hands around my neck and holds for me a long time, cradled in my arms - where she belongs.

She smiles when she traces her fingers over my cheek and the ugly scar that stretches across it.

"I love it. It suits you. It's like a battle scar - from when you saved me from the dragon."

"It turns out I am the dragon." I chuckle. "They've all started calling me the red dragon."

Verity giggles. "I like that too."

The hospital releases Verity the next day, but she is under strict instructions to rest.

The fourth day after her release one of the guards I've hired rushes into my living room. "Boss, Luca A'Vara is here. He wants to see you."

"Alone?"

"He has two guards with him."

"Let him in."

I stand up to wait for my guest.

He walks in with a tight, angry expression on his face.

"Luca." I say calmly. "What can I do for you?"

"I came to tell you face to face that I won't be wanting my daughter back."

"Is that so?"

"You can keep her. You're fucking crazy. Both of you. Fucking psychopathic fucks." He snarls.

"That's not very polite, Luca. Watch your tone."

His jaw muscles ripple and he clenches his fists at his side. After taking a moment to regain control, he takes a deep breath and tries again.

"The point is - it's over. I won't be coming after her or choosing revenge. I just wanted to hear it from your mouth - if I back away - will you back away as well."

I smirk. He's scared.

He realized he was messing with the wrong man.

"As long as you leave us alone - we will leave you alone, Luca." I assure him.

He nods, not making eye contact. "That's settled then. Bye."

"Don't you want to say goodbye to your daughter as well?"

"No. She's your problem now."

He spins on his heels and marches out of my home. The guards follow to escort him off the property.

Verity and I finally have the freedom to live our lives together. Everything we went through, everything we fought for - we have it.

When she is fully healed and back to her feisty, beautiful, spontaneous self, I will tell her about a surprise I have for her.

"We're going to Hawaii?" She asks in excitement.

"Yes. For our proper wedding. We are eloping. Just you and me and the ocean and long stretches of beautiful sandy white beaches. I want to have a proper wedding. If you want to marry me again?"

"I'll marry you a thousand times." She squeals in delight and leaps into my arms.

I laugh as I hold her against me, kissing her passionately.

"You better get packed then. We're leaving tonight."

"Oh my goodness." She squeals again, wiggling out of my arms and running to the bedroom to pack.

This time our wedding is exactly what I would have wanted it to be.

I'm standing beneath an archway covered in pink and white roses. Soft sheer white fabric is moving in the gentle ocean breeze and my bare feet are on smooth white sand right at the edge of the water.

Verity is walking towards me wearing a long white lace and silk dress that hugs tight over her waist and then flares wide, flowing like waves, right down to the ground.

She looks incredible. I'm left speechless, yet my heart is pounding.

She's holding white lilies and pink roses and has a tiara made of rose quartz crystals. She refused to let me buy her another ring. The rose quartz ring from Las Vegas was 'meant to be' as she puts it. She loves it. And that's all that matters to me.

We stand together on the Hawaiian shore. Salty ocean water lapping at our feet while we say our vows. This time - it's perfect.

And when the priest finally says, "I now pronounce you husband and wife." I am already stepping forward to kiss my bride.

We dance beneath the full moon, alone on the beach, in front of our villa.

Then with the slight shine of champagne and amazing foods, I scoop her into my arms to carry her inside.

Our lips meet on the balcony before our hands explore eagerly over our bodies. My cock is throbbing and rock hard against my pants. I need her.

Now.

We've been through so much and come out on the other side - even more in love than before - even more obsessed and crazy for each other.

I lift her up onto the edge of the balustrade and push her dress up over her hips. She moans that beautiful sound as I slip my fingers inside her pussy and rub my thumb over her clit. She's soaked.

She spreads her legs wide and wraps them around my waist while she tugs at my belt. Her tongue teasing my mouth.

I pull the zip open, grabbing her ass and pushing myself up against her. My cock pressing against her pussy.

With my arm wrapped around her back and the crisp night air on our skin, beneath a million glittering stars - I thrust my cock into her tight little pussy and melt at the sound of her gasping pleasure.

She digs her fingers into my back as I fuck her.

Harder and harder.

Pushing against her and gripping her tightly. She moans, not caring if anyone hears, not caring about anything but us.

In this entire world - it's just us.

"You and me against the world." I growl against her ear. "I will never let you out of my sight again, my love."

She spreads her legs wider and tilts her head backwards, letting her long hair fall down her back and exposing her neck to me.

I trace kisses down her soft skin, over her collar bone.

Her nails scratch down my back and her pussy tightens on me.

My cock hardens.

She cries out when she comes. Waves of ecstasy pulsing through her, shaking her body as I cling to her.

I explode inside her, growling with intensity.

"I love you." I whisper against her lips.

"I love you too, Rufino. Now and forever. I never want to be without you. It's you and me against everything. Forever."

Lifting her in my arms I carry her into the villa, because it's our wedding night, and I still want to explore every inch of her.

About the Author

Hannah Rio is from a small town where she grew up reading romance books sent monthly by her book club. She developed a flair for crafting intricate love stories. She understands the delicate dance of heartbreak and joy. As a storyteller, she enjoys contemporary romances with strong, ambitious leading characters working through life's unexpected twists. Her female and male characters can make hearts flutter and eyes tear up. Her novels promise to bring readers back to continue events of new love and passion, secrets, surprises, painful memories, sassy and sweet, grumpy or good-hearted, and adventures with happy ever after endings.

Sign up to her newsletter here:
subscribepage.io/NKn98Z

- instagram.com/hannahrio2024
- amazon.com/author/hannahrio
- linkedin.com/in/hannah-rio-218707307

Also by Hannah Rio

BILLIONAIRES & BABY DADDY'S

His Surprise Baby

Billionaire Baby Daddy Dilemma

Off-Limits Silver Fox Boss

Mistle-Tied To My Silver Fox Boss

MAFIA MEN

Vece Familia Series

Claiming His Mafia Princess

Something Old

Something New

Something Borrowed

Something Blue

A Six Pence For You Shoe

Shattered Revenge - A Vece, Rivas crossover novella

Shattered Pieces Dark Mafia Series (Coming 2025)

King

Queen

Bishop

Knight

Rook

Pawn

HANNAH RIO
Dark heroes with romance at heart

Printed in Great Britain
by Amazon